THE TOWER OF LOVE

T0281765

THE TOWER OF LOVE

RACHILDE

FOREWORD BY MELANIE C. HAWTHORNE
TRANSLATED BY JENNIFER HIGGINS

WAKEFIELD PRESS

CAMBRIDGE, MASSACHUSETTS

This translation © 2024 Wakefield Press

Wakefield Press, P.O. Box 425645, Cambridge, MA 02142

Originally published as *La tour d'amour* in 1899.

This book was set in Garamond Premier Pro, Helvetica Neue Pro, and Marilyn Bold by Wakefield Press. Printed and bound by Versa Press in the United States of America.

ISBN: 978-1-962728-00-3

Available through D.A.P./Distributed Art Publishers
75 Broad Street, Suite 630
New York, New York 10004
Tel: (212) 627-1999
Fax: (212) 627-9484

10   9   8   7   6   5   4   3   2   1

FOREWORD

If the mention of a "tower of love" brings to mind the idea that lighthouses can seem a bit phallic, the reader is thinking along the right lines. But when the *Tour d'amour* (to give it its original French title) by the "decadent" writer Rachilde first appeared in 1899, such Freudian symbolism was far from everyday currency; indeed, Sigmund Freud's masterwork on the interpretation of dreams was published more or less simultaneously with Rachilde's novel (but in German, of course), so the comparisons that might seem clichéd today had not yet percolated into mainstream thought. And it's true that while *The Tower of Love* is undeniably about masculinity, it is also about so much more: it is about the role of language in culture, about the breakdown of civilization, about the evil of misogyny, big themes that grow out of the encounter between two men stationed on a remote lighthouse on a rocky Breton shore, cut off from ordinary, everyday society, where they are forced to confront the limits to human behavior.

The person who produced this troubling look into the depths of depravity was, at this point in her career (she turned forty in 1900), a well-established presence in the Parisian literary scene, known for her depictions of gender-bending dandies, mentally deranged victims of social repression, innocent young women capable of terrifying violence, and scenes of gothic horror. She had not always been such a literary insider: she crashed onto the public stage in the 1880s, riding on the back of the so-called decadent movement and courting scandal for free publicity. But twenty years later she was a semirespectable matron, married to a fixture of the publishing world, and was hosting a famous literary salon. Her situation had become what Simone de Beauvoir would describe as "*bien rangée*" (settled).

The writer who came to be known simply as Rachilde was born Marguerite Eymery in provincial France in 1860. The nearest big town was Périgueux in the Dordogne region, but Rachilde was not born in a big town, or even a small village near a big town, but on a remote estate (though even that description is grandiose) outside the village of Château-L'Evêque, which was called, in local dialect, "the hole" (*Le cros*). Her parents Joseph Eymery and Gabrielle Feytaud were, by local standards, part of the gentry, and their home, sometimes aspirationally described as a "château," was no doubt luxurious for the time and place, but these are relative terms. Certainly, Rachilde had advantages growing up (such as unrestricted access to her grandfather's library), but ultimately, she was a self-starter who forged her own path to success. It would be a challenging climb out of the pit of Le cros to the pinnacles of success in Paris, especially for a woman with literary ambitions in nineteenth-century France.

Rachilde's father was a career officer in a cavalry regiment, but he had started life as a foundling, an abandoned child, so his antecedents remain obscure. But he married well: his bride was accomplished by the standards of the time (she was a talented musician) if somewhat absentminded. Her parents were local figures to be reckoned with in small towns outside Périgueux (Thiviers, Nontron) since her father ran a newspaper (and had a street named after him). This side of the family also had contacts in Paris through extended kinship networks that would eventually help Rachilde get a toehold in the capital. On the other hand, Gabrielle was increasingly prone to mental illness, long undiagnosed, that had a profound influence on Rachilde herself. This feature of her family of origin made her self-reliant from an early age, led to her distrust of mother figures (a recurrent feature of her fiction), caused her ongoing anxiety about her own mental stability, and, in the year after *The Tower of Love* was first published, forced her to have her mother committed to a mental institution (the same one that had housed the Marquis de Sade, noted Rachilde).

Disillusioned as to what she could expect from mothers, Rachilde turned increasingly to her father. Rachilde was an only child, at least an only legitimate one (there were rumors about half siblings among the peasants), and Joseph was bitterly disappointed not to have had a son and heir (not an uncommon attitude in a society that made no secret of its patriarchal bias). He compensated by treating his little daisy (Marguerite means "daisy" in French) as the son he wanted, teaching her to ride, toughening her up. Her introduction to journalism as a teenager was to accompany him on military maneuvers and report on them for the newspaper. But her father's approval came at a price: there was no crying in Joseph's world, no room for emotion, and indeed, after his experience as a prisoner of war in the 1870 Prussian War left him deaf, very little room for communication of any kind.

At times, Rachilde and her father ended up in complete opposition. Wolves were a problem in rural France: they posed a threat to farmers and their livestock and were considered a pest to be exterminated. Joseph was a leader of the wolf patrol, hunting them down, and dispatching them according to the cruel custom of the time. A wolf wasn't worth wasting a bullet on, so instead the captured animal would be pinned down by a stake driven through the leg and left to die. But Rachilde was on the side of the wolf. Her childhood playmates had been animals (few other socially acceptable children being available), and she was an animal sympathizer throughout her life. She even thought of herself as a kind of lone wolf—and claimed to be a werewolf—and was drawn by compassion if not tribal loyalty to the defense of such an underdog. She followed the wolf patrol, attempted to free the stricken victims of her father's purges, and thus undid her father's work (see the account she gives in *Le parc du mystère*).

Rachilde's father also hated "scribblers" (*des plumitifs*), even though (or perhaps because) he had married into a family of them, so Rachilde's literary aspirations were not encouraged by this man of action. When Rachilde wanted to launch her career in Paris, it was her mother who paved the way, her mother who had connections, her mother who had a little *pied à terre*; Joseph stayed behind on the country estate, living the life of the country squire, while the women got on with it in the salons. Rachilde's connection to her father was thus a complicated one. It has even been suggested that their relationship might have involved physical and/or sexual abuse. But what is certain is that these family dynamics shaped Rachilde's understanding of masculinity and femininity. To Rachilde, the feminine and maternal represented weakness, vulnerability, and betrayal. Masculinity came with cruelty, sadism, and discipline, but in a world that imposed a choice between being the victim or the victimizer, Rachilde had enough instinct for self-preservation that she could not consent to side with the victims. She identified with the masculine: especially when she was launching her career, she referred to herself as a "man" of letters, cross-dressed as a man (which required special police permission at the time), and sported short hair, at least briefly, leading some today to read her through a queer lens. She overtly rejected the constraints of traditional female roles offered by her time. She blamed women for accepting their second-class status (she didn't think that women deserved the vote, for example), and declared herself not a feminist (if being a feminist meant championing women like her mother and grandmother, an important qualification). She embodied the exceptional woman, the one who could make it (or fake it) in a man's world.

This apprenticeship began when she was still a teenager living at home in the provinces. Her parents had embraced spiritism, a popular craze at the time (and an entertaining parlor game when there was little else in the way of distraction). This was an enabling medium (pun intended) for a girl with narrative aspirations. She invented the name Rachilde at this time, claiming it was the name of a Swedish gentleman who spoke through her. This persona turned out to be the perfect cover: the name could function either as a first name or a last (some people referred to her as Madame Rachilde, for example); it looked morphologically feminine (combining the name Rachel with the French "soft" -e ending), but at the same time it was supposed to be the name of a man, so it confused gender categories in a convenient way. And the pose that Rachilde was merely the medium for giving voice to another was a ventriloquist act that shielded Rachilde from accusations that plagued other women writers (that they were hysterical and monstrous, only wanted publicity, were bluestockings, etc.). The only disadvantage proved, much later, to be that to the occupying Nazis in World War II, the name looked Jewish, so they put her books on the proscribed "Otto" list. But in 1870s Dordogne, the future writer who was still known as Marguerite had found her path. She could make up stories and present them as someone else's work; she was just the messenger. She sought a wider audience than family and neighbors by riding her horse to Périgueux, sometimes dressed as a girl, sometimes as a boy, and selling the stories to the local newspaper. What the editor made of this twin tag team is not known, but the device of the male-female double became another running theme in Rachilde's work. And to add a further twist to her formation as a literary figure, Rachilde claimed that when she read aloud the stories that appeared under a pseudonym in the local newspaper to her family at home, her father never realized that the author of the tales was seated right next to him.

So it was as "Rachilde" that Marguerite made her debut in Paris, and took the public by storm with her brash self-presentation as a kind of virginal slut, a purveyor of scandalous stories about effeminate men and masculine women, always a reliable source of sensationalism. She rapidly became famous as the author of a gender-bending novel, *Monsieur Vénus* (1884), which was banned (but easily obtained from neighboring Belgium). It was not her first novel, but the first in a series of *succès de scandale*.

In Paris, she allied herself with avant-garde literary cliques, especially the emerging decadent movement. The humiliating military defeat in 1870 prompted a lot of national soul-searching. The republican ideals of the 1789 revolution had encouraged France to position itself as the modern heir to Rome, but as the anniversary of that revolution approached, there was a growing sense that France was no longer living up to that virtuous image, that it was instead in decline. France had gone soft, had passed its peak ripeness, and was beginning to rot, to "deliquesce." But a younger generation saw the criticism that they were decadent as an identity to be reclaimed, and they embraced the label as a sign of superior sensibility, joined by Rachilde. By the end of the 1880s, she had a string of controversial but much-discussed novels to her name, and she settled into the role that would carry her through the next decade, leading up to the turn of the century and *The Tower of Love*. She married Alfred Vallette, one of the founding members of a major literary review that went on to become a powerhouse in French publishing, the *Mercure de France*. It was very likely a marriage of convenience—Rachilde was pregnant when they married, and Vallette may not have been the father of the child—but it was an arrangement that suited them for life, making them a celebrity couple, arbiters of literary taste, and hosts to the literary who's who of the day at their Tuesday salon. In the 1890s, Rachilde would continue to write prolifically, consolidating her reputation. She also branched out into avant-garde theater (France was discovering Strindberg and Ibsen), writing her own symbolist plays, becoming a "gatekeeper" as member of a reading committee selecting works for production, and making theater history through her role in bringing Alfred Jarry's unique play *Ubu roi* to the stage.

Rachilde was already a successful novelist when *The Tower of Love* appeared, then. It was first published "in house" by the Mercure de France company that Alfred Vallette had helped to found and that he led until his death in 1935. The novel's popularity meant that it was reprinted several times during Rachilde's lifetime (she died in 1953 following a fall), and its reputation as one of her most accomplished works led to several posthumous editions (as well as an audio book version).

The novel represented something of a departure for Rachilde in being set in Brittany, the rugged northwestern coast of France, rather in the more familiar (to Rachilde) Dordogne area where she chose to situate much of her fiction. The reason for this choice might be found in events in the years leading up to the composition of the work: there was a major shipwreck in June of 1896 that drew much public attention. The Drummond Castle was headed back to England from South Africa, but owing to human error it struck a rock off the westernmost tip of Brittany. The ship sank within just four minutes, taking with it an estimated 242 souls (passengers and crew); only three survived. There was no lighthouse at the time to warn the ship that it was dangerously off course, but shortly after the accident, construction of one began (it would be called La Jument, or "the Mare"). Rachilde drew on press coverage of these events when drafting her novel (the Drummond Castle becomes the Dermond-Nestle, for example). The press was also led to comment on the isolated life and difficult working conditions of lighthouse keepers, often cut off from the rest of society for long periods by bad weather, conditions that inspired all kinds of speculation in what might be called "the literature of lighthouses." In Rachilde's imagination such isolation offered the perfect conditions for a mental breakdown, which lies at the core of her story.

A somewhat unusual aspect of the wreck of the Drummond Castle was the response of the coastal communities where the bodies and cargo washed up or were retrieved. France and Britain often clashed on the high seas, so it was not obvious how the Breton fishing communities would react to a British loss. Added to the national animus, there were rules—unwritten but widely acknowledged—about the rights to the "windfall" booty that washed ashore. By extension, those who subscribed to the "finders, keepers" philosophy were also sometimes tempted, it was said, to go one step further to improve their chances of such a lucky find by deliberately luring ships into dangerous waters (turning off lighthouse lanterns that would warn ships away or offering misleading lights to bring ships closer to reefs, for example). In *The Tower of Love*, Rachilde wove in allusions to this popular folklore about so-called wreckers. There were plenty of rumors about such suspicious behavior (the British composer Ethel Smyth premiered an opera about one such Cornish community in 1906), but Rachilde homes in on the psychology of one particular character who is less than dutiful. In the end, the Breton villagers who had to clean up after the Drummond Castle, shocked by the human loss, seem to have behaved quite decently; the same cannot be said for the lighthouse keepers in Rachilde's novel.

The dark secret of the lighthouse is gradually discovered by the first-person narrator, Jean Maleux, who comes as an apprentice to work with the reclusive (and repulsive) Mathurin Barnabas. The French reader knows from Jean's name, which in French has connotations of misfortune (*malheur*) and unhappiness (*malheureux*), that the lighthouse job is probably not going to work out well for him (any more than it did for his predecessor who died "in an accident"), but the full extent of the toll that the prolonged contact with Barnabas takes on Jean's psyche only gradually becomes apparent. Jean's malaise takes on a metaphysical dimension through Rachilde's poetic descriptions of the rugged Breton landscape. If the lighthouse embodies the male principle, the sea (*la mer*) represents the feminine, but this force of nature is anything but a passive or peaceful one, hurling itself against the rocks, lashing angrily at the tower, and putting the men's very lives at risk. Is it any wonder that such a wild and dangerous entity engenders hostility in men who experience a need to control and tame it—with violence if necessary. And since the French for "sea" and "mother" are homonyms (*mer* and *mère*), fin-de-siècle misogyny spills over into what Freud would characterize as the Elektra complex, an identification with the father accompanied by hostility toward the mother, the very features that recall the dynamics of Rachilde's family of origin.

The story of *The Tower of Love* brings us full circle. Despite the superficial differences (a setting in Brittany rather than the Périgord, a male rather than female narrator), a familiar constellation takes shape in which Rachilde plumbs the depths of human aberrations through a powerful story told with bold and evocative language. Rachilde's contemporaries found this to be one of her best novels, and thanks to this translation, Anglophone readers, too, can now enjoy this pillar of European fin-de-siècle literature.

Melanie C. Hawthorne

THE TOWER OF LOVE

I

When I showed up for the third time, I was shown straight into the office. For once, the powers that be didn't make me wait for hours on their hard benches while they forgot I was even there. I can still see the room: yellow paint, bluebottles buzzing around the inkwells, and hot, even though they'd opened the window onto the harbor where boats bobbed like ducks in the strong west wind.

I found myself in front of two gentlemen: one skinny, one short and fat.

The short fat one put on his officer's cap, bristling with brocade.

The skinny one inspected his nails.

They shuffled some papers about, not saying anything, looking at me narrowly as though they were inspecting a tun for a leak.

I was still standing, very straight.

I was scared.

It reminded me of the day I started my first sea voyage. I couldn't lift my eyes from my shoes. I'd polished them specially but my toes poked through. Luckily these gentlemen must have thought well enough of my clothes. I was wearing a brown regulation overcoat, nice and shiny, over canvas trousers with leather gaiters, and I'd just been to a bric-à-brac shop in Brest and bought myself a handsome blue beret with a pompom the size of a cabbage.

They shuffled and shuffled, I turned my beret round and round in my hands . . . It could have gone on forever, but then the short fat one with all the brocade, the boss, said:

"Are you Jean Maleux?"

"I have the pleasure of being so, yes," I said very politely, thinking I shouldn't talk any old how in this grand place.

"We've chosen you, my boy, from ten applicants, and I hope we shan't come to regret our choice. You are appointed to the *Ar-Men*."

Ah! The *Ar-Men*. I took a deep breath, as though they'd lifted a sixty-kilo weight off my belly. I had no idea what lay in store for me. I was so pleased I could have danced a jig there in front of them. No more being shunted around, no more apprenticeships. I was set up: my own master, state lodgings, a respectable post, and no one bothering me.

"You're not yet thirty," said the skinny one. "That's young."

He was stroking his beard and still inspecting his nails. He seemed to be looking for fleas to kill.

"I'll be older soon enough," I replied with a laugh.

"You'll grow older very quickly on the *Ar-Men*," said the brocaded one, who wasn't laughing, perhaps because he knew what he was talking about. "We're taking you on because of the *other one*, already out there, who's deteriorating. He's very experienced but he needs a lad to help him. We have to send supplies out to the *Ar-Men*. Did you know that, young man?"

I didn't know anything, except that I was happy.

"Oh!" said I, in all innocence. "You can stop in one place in the sea, or you can move around in it—it's wet and salty either way. I'm not afraid of hard work, and I've seen worse."

"You sailed the Levant ports as a stoker, with Captain Dartigues?"

"Yes Sir."

And I was on my guard straight away.

He was looking through my papers; I caught sight of my school certificate and my last logbook in his hand.

"You were a hothead, by all accounts?"

I knew it! . . . The story of my quarrel with the second engineer, that cursed day when I got so drunk. It just goes to show: one night of carousing and they'll never let you forget it.

"Perhaps, Captain, when I've had a drop too much. It went no further than a couple of lashes with the rope's end. The other fellow admitted he was as tipsy as I was. We'd been away a long time and, well, we were going to see the ladies. I don't mean to offend, but that always fires you up . . . I got more of a keelhauling than I deserved . . ." I bit my tongue and quickly added, "I mean, they acted fair."

"Well, well," the thin one said. "Here are your papers. They're in order. You'll take up your post tomorrow. By the way, the man you're replacing, old Mathurin Barnabas's previous companion, died . . . in an *accident*, and we had to have a little inquiry, but the old man came out of it honorably. He's a decent man; I'm just telling you so you know. No mentioning the . . . *accident*, eh?"

"It all sounds fair," I answered. I was confused.

I didn't know anything about anything back then, it would seem. Anyway, what did all their dealings with the old man matter to me? I'd come back from China and all I wanted was to stop sailing. Seven years spent sneezing in the holds of their ships was plenty for me. Now it was time to settle down in my own little place, my port in a storm. Great God! If only I'd hanged myself from the highest mast of the last ship I'd stoked . . .

Next, they told me about the pay. A good sum for not much work. That should've made me suspicious. They told me to tie my bundle of belongings up tight, as though I were going diving with it, and to be ready the next day bright and early.

The skinny one added, sweet but sharp:

"Let's have no carousing, no women, my boy. We want serious people, *with enough experience of life not to miss leaving it behind*, and you've thought about the responsibility you're taking on, I hope?"

I'd never thought about anything from the moment I was born. They didn't half annoy me, this pair, with their fussing. Like buzzing bluebottles; it sent me to sleep. It wasn't as though I looked like a weak little girl. They pointed out that I was privileged, chosen above ten others because of my face, the trusty face of a loner. I had a poor, skinny body, like all stokers, hardened by the breath of the fire. I had nothing to regret, having nothing to leave. Anyone could see that.

To top it all off, the short fat one patted me on the shoulder as he showed me the door and murmured, as though he were praying for a dying man:

"Take courage, my boy, and remember that you hold the destinies of great ships in your hands."

I almost replied:

"Small ones too, Captain."

But I wanted to show that I knew how to behave, so I just backed out of the room, beret in hand, saying:

"It'll make a man of me."

There was no going back now. They don't mess around in that part of the navy: once you're in, you're in. You can't go crying to them later, saying it's making you sick as a dog.

"Jean Maleux," I said to myself as I walked away, "This is your chance. Save everything you earn until you've done your time. Twenty-five years of service isn't so hellish when you're pampered like that. No superior officer looking over your shoulder, complete freedom, and the old wolf won't eat you up—you're his crutch in old age. We've set sail now, my boy, come what may! Jean, you were born under a lucky star."

I didn't doubt my luck, not for a second.

The next day there was a slight wind, milder than the day before, and the sea was like oil.

We set off.

We left Brest to go and supply the *Ar-men* in a vessel called the *Saint-Christophe*, a little steam tender replacing the *Georges-Alfred*, which had recently been spoiled (in these parts, *spoiled* doesn't mean a splash of mud on a woman's skirt or a tear where someone's walked on it . . . it means the boat split in two on a rock and was lost with all hands).

The night before, I'd wandered the streets near the port, regretting that I couldn't go and say my goodbyes to the fairer sex because my last centime had gone on a new cap. I held on tight to my bundle, tied up just as they'd told me, and felt very melancholy.

The captain of the *Saint-Christophe* sized me up, made me sign a few more bits of paper, and flicked through my logbook. Then he told me to go down and keep the stoker company, because he could tell from the look of me that I knew a thing or two about stoking.

"All right, shipmate, if you say so . . . but this'll be the last time. I've had enough of coal. I'm about to get myself my own house, a real one, on dry land, and I'll sit and watch all your silly little cockleshells jigging on the water."

I'd dreamed all my life of living in one of those beautiful State-owned towers, and the honor was being handed to me on a plate. Honor indeed . . . they had me in their net, caught like a porpoise . . . and I so conceited . . . How stupid I was.

Now I've learned some wisdom and right thinking, enough to make me mad, and it can't do me any good. It's too late.

I could only see water through the porthole in the hold, but I knew the places off by heart. We were rounding the Islet of the Capuchins and the *Tévennec* lighthouse to reach the *Ar-Men*, passing by the *Sein* lighthouse and the *Pont-de-Sein* reef.

The chief stoker, a decent sort, gave me a cup of brandy, English stuff that knocked me off balance a bit because I'd forgotten to eat.

I'd make up for that once we got to *my home*, so I drained the cup and tried to get him to talk.

"Is this just a trial or have you really got the job?" he asked, resting his chin on his shovel.

"I've finished the trial, thank God, my friend. Everything's shipshape and I'm going there to stay, for my whole life, I hope."

"*Ah*," he said, pensively.

And I didn't notice his tone of voice.

I prattled on to my heart's content. I was proud as a peacock, with my bundle tied to my belt, my old clothes, my papers, my books, all my precious things. I chattered away all by myself, pratting on about how the Chinese had fat bellies because they ate too much rice. The assistant stoker listened, nodding his head, his ears pricked up for instructions from above.

Nobody, I remember now, laughed at my jokes about my flat belly, or fat Chinese ones.

I even remember the chief stoker once gesturing to me to be quiet as he crouched over his machinery.

Another time he mumbled:

"He got lucky, that Mathurin Barnabas."

And he exchanged glances with his assistant.

Who was this Mathurin? My brain was well and truly stewed.

At ten o'clock we reached the *Ar-Men*. I could tell because we were being tossed about. The sea's always rough around there. It's like a current hitting the column of a bridge, except there's no bridge here and you have to watch out for the slightest impact, as though you were in a boat made of glass.

They called my name through the loud hailer.

I scrambled up and found myself looking at . . . *my retirement home*.

The *Ar-Men* lighthouse soared up right next to the *Saint-Christophe*, skirted by the ocean's foaming gobbets. The waves tore themselves apart at its base, shrieking and slavering in their desire to demolish it. I never thought it would be so huge, such a colossus. I'd already seen a model of it in the apprentice manager's office, a toy version only as long as your finger and covered in little silver ladders. They used it as a paperweight and it sat there, looking no more impressive than the others. You could light it, apparently, just like a pipe. Only in real life it wasn't so funny. The docking crane and its pass rope veiled its face, like an enormous spider web. Perched on a rock that nobody had ever managed to set foot on before, it seemed to hold there by a miracle, so wide and high that you felt proud of the strength of the men who'd put it there. Thirty-six years of work and a good dose of corpses! The monster was fat from devouring so many workers. Its rump, rising out of the water, shone as though coated with a viscous substance; the paved base, running around the bottom of the tower, was smooth as marble. It could have been the front steps of a town hall, it was so white and pretty, but all around, when the waves collapsed back in on themselves, you could see holes, like old holes in decaying teeth, and it smelled of the sea: sour, with a hint of rotten blood.

We set off the signals and the docking crane was lowered. The monster deigned to hold out its paw. We were given a few buoys: it took nearly an hour to spear them, the sea was so truculent.

"Must be lovely in a storm," I remarked.

The lads hauling the cable muttered:

"Just you wait."

At that moment I remember I was thinking:

"I'm somebody. They're doing things for me."

I was full of myself, no doubt about it, and full of respect for my position.

The poor little standard-issue navy steamboat was shaking about on its motors, enough to make you dizzy; the waves pranced along its sides and some of the fiercest came and stuck their tongues out at us, dabbing our noses with saliva.

Now the hoist was loaded with the basket of provisions, a heavy wire cage full of good things, well wrapped in tar cloth. We were about to get a soaking. We hoisted hard. The man directing the whole maneuver gave us some thunderous looks. In any case, the sea was making such a racket that we needed to see the glint in the good comrade's eyes or we'd never have understood the orders. Despite all our precautions, the package took an enormous gulp. It was as though someone was pulling it from below us while we were hoisting up. And we wondered if it would end up falling into the lighthouse's gullet, with its round door yawning wide from far off like a snake's maw.

The basket made it, somehow or other: we saw an old man, presumably Mathurin Barnabas, rush to grasp it, an old man looking more like a bird of prey, walking bent double, his arms dragging like tattered wings.

After the basket it was my turn.

I was still sitting on the bridge of the *Saint-Christophe*, staring stupidly at the sea as it hurled its vulgar insults at me. The open air wasn't clearing my head. I still thought I was the lord of a corkscrew-shaped manor that was going to pierce the sky simply to make showers of English liquor flow from it. And I had to climb up it. I cried:

"Heave! Heave ho!"

I'd clamber up the clouds and then bang, I'd hit my head on our heavenly Father's ceiling.

It was my turn.

The man in charge of the boat, the officer with the glittering eyes, gave me a dig in the ribs.

"What's it to be, my boy, with your hands or in the sling . . . ?"

I replied, piqued:

"With my hands, of course."

Does a lighthouse keeper do his work sitting down? What did he take me for?

"Put the lifebelt on him," said the captain tersely.

That sobered me up a bit. Perhaps I shouldn't have boasted.

The hoists we'd used for training weren't much like those on the *Ar-Men*. They put the lifebelt on me.

"I'm no landlubber!" I grumbled. "I've seen plenty like this in China."

Then I looked at *my home* and gave it a respectful nod. It seemed bigger and loomed toward me all of a sudden.

The sky was blue behind a reddish mist, and the wind had turned sour, whipping, salty.

So was I going to fly off on a swing, like a little girl?

I heard the wail of the siren. It tore through the air like the shriek of a woman getting her throat slit.

I knew what it was . . . but it still gave me the shivers.

"You haven't eaten, I hope?" the captain asked me.

"Me? I'm dying of hunger," I replied, trying to laugh.

"So much the better!"

And they pass me the cable: I fasten myself on and turn around, pushing away from the bridge with my feet.

I turn more quickly, clinging on, head spinning . . .

The siren bellows more loudly, drilling into my ears. As though it's got it in for me. I'm dazed. It's not like the practice exercises. This is far more serious, because of the siren and because I'm tipsy.

I spin and spin. My stomach turns too, alas! I have an extraordinary urge to let go of everything and meet my watery end. But in spite of myself, I hang on.

I fly, I leap, I turn . . . I'm shaken as though by a giant fist. I can no longer see. Either I'm drunker than ever, or the boat and the lighthouse are spinning around me; sometimes the boat is as small as a walnut, sometimes the lighthouse stretches thin like a church candle.

"Jean Maleux, you're done for!" snarls the far-off siren.

I swing down again . . .

My legs are freezing. I'm right in the water. It's coming into my mouth now. That's it, that's the end of Jean Maleux! No point swimming, I'd be smashed against the rock . . .

. . . And here I am dragging myself up again. Now I'm fifteen meters above the waves. I see the face of an old woman coming toward me, a horrible old woman's face with red eyelids. Who is this hag? I never knew my grandmother or even my mother. Am I already dead and seeing ghosts? I'm slipping down again, I'm touching the water, I'm cold up to my chest. I bob there, hanging pitifully, *paddling* like a little boy. I'm stunned, overcome, desperate; I'd sell my soul to the devil to get out of this water lashing my behind so cruelly. The wild waves crash harder around the monster. I feel as though I'm dying with hordes of others, as we shall all die on the last day of the world when the dead will burst from their coffins. I tip back my head to glimpse the sky, but there's no more sky, only the monster, the lighthouse that grows and swells and looms up almost touching my stomach. I feel as though I'm lifting it and it's crushing me, this formidable, naked lighthouse, its green lamp glowing through the white sheets of spray. It opens its gullet . . . just a gullet, with no eye sockets. It's blind, but it'll swallow me just the same. So much for all my conceit. I start shouting, my hands bleeding from grasping this rope. I'm going to let go for good . . .

The wild old woman appears again. She bends and holds out her arms like featherless wings.

"Ho! Heave! Heave up! Ho! . . ."

It's as though this siren were singing a death lament inside the tower.

I plunge straight into its black gullet.

I've arrived.

I've been eaten!

But I've lost consciousness. I slump down like a bundle of laundry.

And I can still see that infernal old woman's face.

"It's her! It's a death's head, by God! It's death! . . ."

II

The old man was sitting opposite me, his head bowed. At last, he said:

"How many steps? There's . . . there's . . . two hundred and ten, *not counting the others.*"

When it came down to it, this old man was my superior, far more experienced than I was, and I had to listen to him respectfully. But he struggled to get his words out, and something about that opening remark gave me an odd feeling, either because of the darkness all around us, or because of the tone of his voice. It sang or cried, hard to say which, and he paused on all the *e* sounds with quavering emphasis. It was as though someone was pulling it out of him with tongs. I couldn't laugh because I still had a stomach full of salt water. I'd nearly drowned when they hoisted me over, and I wasn't feeling so cock-a-hoop anymore, all things considered.

Night was rising around us.

At sea, night doesn't come down from above, it rises from the waves as though the water had turned into clouds, an upside-down sky.

So I was submerged in bitterness, and I felt very alone despite the old man's presence.

We were eating in the middle of the *Ar-Men*'s small, round dining room, which in daylight was lit by its arched door opening onto the paved base of the lighthouse, and in the evening by an oil lamp hanging from the ceiling, a candle stub with a zinc cover that smoked so vigorously that you could barely see what you were putting in your mouth. There was an old wooden table between us with a loaf on it, and some ham, a jug of cider, and a bottle of rum. No soup because the place had no stove. We lived off a load of rancid preserved food that the navy wanted to get rid of, and the old man bought his little drinks as luxuries with his own pennies. By way of crockery we had, all in all, two big tin bowls and two horn-handled knives. All sturdy stuff. You could bet the wind wouldn't carry off the cutlery. Our stools were held tight to the table legs by lengths of twisted rope. There was a portrait of Napoleon on the wall, and one of our latest President, alongside a big calendar with all the tide dates underlined lots of times in ink. In a black frame, behind glass, hung our task chart: duty periods, low water times, watch times, rest times, and how to repair the lantern mechanism if it was damaged when there was *no available help*, with endless drawings and instructions, stuff we both had to know by heart. A Breton clock, a true Breton creation, fumbled its way through the hours, making a noise like a wooden broom sweeping gravel; but next to it sat a navy clock in a double crystal case, with weights, counterweights and all, a silver service made of tin and full of mystery, where you could lose minutes gazing at your reflection, so that the local clock, although always slow, caught up with you at the turn of the circle. The Paris navy clock told you the day, the month, the year, the tide times, all the equinox tides and the great winds, and even had a picture of a little sinking ship that jiggled up and down when the sea was getting rough. Except . . . it didn't always jiggle at the right time, as I was able to confirm later.

As I gazed around, inspecting that poor excuse for a room, the old man just stared at the floor, stone paving cemented onto ten feet of rock, and didn't say a word, seemed almost deaf, chewing so hard you could hear the sound of his jaws over the sweeping of the clock.

I turned his phrase over in my mind:

"*Not counting the others*"?

This lighthouse had two hundred and ten steps from its rocky feet to its glass head. So where did the *other steps* go?

"The others? There's surely not a cellar here? You don't mean the outside rungs, I suppose? The ones up to the docking crane?"

He twisted his mouth, like a toothless old lady's, into a "no."

By my reckoning, and I was a pretty good reckoner in those days, I could picture all two hundred and ten of them from a bird's eye view . . . but I *never* got an explanation of those other ones.

The old man was permanently stooped, bent over like an animal as though he'd been born that way. He got up eventually, but looked as though he were still sitting down. His long, broad hands were like two paddles, almost dragging on the floor, and he began to gather things up from it most meticulously. First, he picked up his breadcrumbs, then mine, ferreting underneath his stool to get at the little lumps of fat from the ham that he'd spat out as he ate. Once he'd scraped everything up, he put it in a heap on the edge of the table and, with a backhand swipe, sent it flying toward the door, outside. Then he poured himself a half glass of rum, downed it, nodded his head slowly, as though someone had asked his opinion, and didn't offer me a drop. That offended me.

Half drowned, barely dried out, my stomach not to rights, I'd have liked a more comfortable dessert. I was used to the hot soups in the canteen at the navy school. They weren't very thick, but they were hot, still bubbling even in the bowl, so they chased the sea water out of our minds. Anyway, I'd come to this house, which was partly mine, and I thought I deserved a warmer welcome. One man's as good as the next. True, I was younger, but there were only the two of us between the sky and the rock, and that made us brothers despite the difference in age.

Still, I pretended not to care.

Perhaps he didn't want to get to know me today.

Maybe tomorrow.

For now, we had our duties to see to.

I helped him put away our little stock of things. The knives and the tin bowls went in a drawer, the bread was wrapped in a cloth that had once been white, and the ham we put at the back of a cupboard with the oil cans. The old man kept his rum inside the clock, in a back corner that the pendulum didn't reach. It was his property, and there were no rules against keeping a bit of grog.

To show my goodwill, I gave the barometers a careful examination. I remarked that they were showing some swell on the waves, and pointed at the maps, showing all the scientific terms I knew. He listened, trying to hear what I was saying. His face was like a little old lady's, dead from having drunk too much, and a mocking expression crept across it. He went over to the door, an oval door like whale's gullet, and, to my horror, vomited onto the lighthouse's pale base. Straightening up again, he turned and held out his right hand, spreading it out wide to let the sea spray dampen it. Then he licked it carefully.

I watched, flabbergasted.

I later learned that this was his way of gauging the state of the wind in a bad spell of weather.

I pretended to approve, keeping up appearances. How clever old people are! And we walked a few times around the base.

At that time in the evening, it was a frightening sight: two poor little men next to that stone giant, on a godforsaken rock. Furious waves tackled it crosswise, almost toppling it from its rump, drooling spray that fell like snow onto the paving slabs on the north side. You could hear the battering of the waves' cannons, shaking the whole edifice and making it vibrate like a tin trumpet. Now I understood why the chairs in the dining room were tied down! In a storm the water sucked so hard that it dragged anything that wasn't held down outside. Christian souls too, no doubt . . .

On very blustery nights we couldn't go out. We managed to stay upright, through habit, but we could feel ourselves sucked down from the depths, which opened up in a great spiral to help us slip easily down into the belly of the sea.

The base was white and shining, soapy under your heels, going from a milky color to the delicate nuance of the water itself, the transparent greenish white of thickly enameled porcelain, which finally merged with the waves.

The sea would rise up, clambering higher and higher, then pause for an endless moment level with the top steps before falling back, exhausted, only to rear up again five seconds later, even more furiously. It executed this hostile maneuver right in front of you and there was no defense against it; no parapet to block its entry, no iron grill to break its teeth. It climbed up and sank its fangs in, made itself at home, but an invisible rampart dominated its anger: the low water mark fixed by the engineers, in their wisdom. The sea couldn't get higher than that, and if they let it get that far it was only to tease it more.

Still, the lighthouse did have the look of a sinking ship's mast, and you felt as though you were being carried off in all directions at once.

Oh yes, the architect must have been a proud man. I was to learn later that there'd been three of them, and that during the thirty-six years of work, two had met their deaths on the job.

The old man smoked a pipe that evening, as the weather was fine, if you can call it fine when there's snow, salt, and rain pelting down, with smudgy stars peering through the holes in a tattered sky.

Once the pipe was smoked, he went inside to light a lamp and go to bed, taking no more notice of me.

There was another room down at the bottom, his bedroom, round like an egg sitting next to another egg. His bed was there, two wrack mattresses on two iron x-shaped frames, a wardrobe full of old tarred rags and a shelf of dusty books. He didn't show me anything, just rolled into a ball without taking off his overcoat or even the heavy leather boots that made his lower half look like a seal, and shuffled up against the wall, muttering something or other all the while.

I stood at his door, my own lantern in my hand, not knowing what to do with myself. I knew what my task was, to be on watch up at the top while he snored down here; but I didn't think it companionable of him to assign the first night's watch to me, when I'd drunk more salt water than rum. As a rule, you show the new man the ropes and give him a few slaps on the back for encouragement; you give him a bit of guidance to whet his appetite for the work.

But there was none of that, nothing but a snort like a pig.

"What a brute!" I thought to myself.

And, closing his door, I headed up the spiral staircase that began opposite his bed.

"Two hundred and ten, not one more," I said when I reached the top.

I'd climbed up all in one breath, very familiar with the treacherous twists of lighthouse staircases. If you go slowly, it turns your stomach.

But this one, an abominable thing, had no air vents (or they'd been stopped up because the old man was afraid of rheumatism), and was stiflingly hot, so it felt like walking toward a fire. You were sucked up by a mouth of light at the very top, and the walls, which were wet on the outside, gave off warm vapor on the inside.

My bedroom, where the lad who perished by *accident* had slept, was on the top landing, an oval hole as hot as an oven because it was so close to the lamps. You couldn't see a thing in there. Everything was red, a dark red plunged further into darkness every so often when the regulating discs passed over the wicks.

There I had my bed, two wrack mattresses on two iron x-shaped frames, a couple of rough sheets, three blankets, one of which was tarred, my ragged, sodden clothes, a few papers, and some books.

Above my bed, with all the conceit of a young man who's . . . not so bad to look at, I pinned a photograph of a Moorish girl I'd met during my time on coasters in those parts. I began to breathe a little in that inferno and started noting down my first impressions in my logbook. It wasn't obligatory, but they'd told me that since the old man had *lost the knack of writing*, it would be wise to mention important things: the number of vessels passing by, their flag and their speed, especially when there were rip currents. I had a little folding table, fixed to the floor like everything else, a wrought-iron bookshelf where the binoculars sat, and all the usual wickie's paraphernalia. I might add that it stank of paraffin and that there was a distinct lack of rum. A narrow glass corridor, corseted with solid steel girders, led to the lantern, set in the center of a stone hemisphere. The lantern could be turned by means of powerful machinery, with the keeper immobile next to it, or he could risk going round by the gallery, when that was possible. The wind raged constantly on the crenelated balcony, and every few steps it threatened to throw you over once and for all.

It was autumn, and things were deteriorating. For all that old Mathurin's *damp finger method* observations predicted a fine spell, there was a rough wind; for good weather, it was a changeable good. And it was choppy! It wouldn't be any use them trying to come to us and bring supplies the next day. It wasn't hard to understand why the navy insisted on us having provisions enough for *five months*. I was idiotic enough to open one of the glass panes: I got a barrage of salty slaps in the face, and it took all my force to push the pane back into place.

They say that one night the hurricane lifted the lantern clean off.

The light itself, a fixed lamp, was constructed from three levels of wicks, and each section gave as much light as a chandelier at Christmas. The engineers were planning to adapt it for electricity, but for now it ran on mineral oil, like all good kitchen lamps. It had three rows of overlapping reflectors like an Archimedes mirror, and the rays escaped from it in three pinkish-yellow beams that faded to a delicate shade of sulfur before falling into the sea, far off, hazy and almost white, the white of a shroud.

Sure enough: it started well, it ended badly.

There are new inventions that mean the beam stays the same shade until it hits the water, which avoids tricks of the light. We weren't rich on the *Ar-Men*, apparently. Inventions are always expensive medicine.

The triple framework of crystal and steel that protects the lights from the wind doesn't always defend them from the greatest of all dangers: the *bird-stone*. A bird as big as your fist comes bombing along, crashes into the lantern, goes through all the panes and falls dead on a wick that either fizzles out or turns black. All the sea birds—petrels, gulls, passing cranes, winter ducks, swifts— they all whirl around the lantern cage and end up with more than a few ruffled feathers, especially when it's stormy, but none of them has the same heroism, and none abandon themselves so fully to the lashing of the water as this species. Only a few learned people know its name. We just call it the *bird-stone*, plain and simple. It shoots straight from God's catapult, as big as your fist, and it often means the loss of a ship.

I stood on the gallery, looking out over the parapet, and listened for a moment to the moaning of the harp of ropes hanging from the crane hoist. Everything was behaving admirably. Our lamps glowed high and pure; there was plenty of fuel in the reservoir. I could go to sleep, that was certain. The old man would get up, because when you've been in the habit for twenty years, you do your job without even meaning to.

I got into bed with all my clothes on (I was so tired!) carefully closing the door that opened onto the lamp. It was still as bright as day in my room. The glare and enormous heat came through the cracks in the wood. The light came in strings that danced and leaped, tickling my cheeks like bees' wings. It disturbed me so much that I turned my face to the wall. There, I saw the photograph of my old flame, the little Moorish girl, and I began to laugh with her a little, despite it all, as I dozed off. Was I really sleeping or was I dreaming wide awake? Either way, I heard a woman singing . . . !

It was very quiet at first, a purr coming from the bottom of the tower, a damsel seemingly coming up the stairs humming a waltz. Then it swelled and I heard words. Such a doleful voice, such an afflicted voice, a voice to dissolve your innards. It pained me to hear it. I tried to wake up fully. I couldn't do it; I was tied by those damned strings of light. I was hot, sweating.

It was still climbing up.

My door opened, the one on the stairs side. I saw the old man come in on silent feet. I unstuck my eyelids. He walked with trailing arms, as usual. His head was well wrapped in a cap with woolen earflaps, and two thick tresses of hair fell down over his cheeks.

The old man had hair at night then, did he? Strange.

I sat up and called out:

"Well, friend, the wind's settling in! We'll both watch together this first evening, shall we?"

He said nothing.

The woman's voice followed him as he went. I heard a snatch of a song that would lead Satan to the cemetery, and, sticking my little finger into my earhole to clear it out, thinking a scrap of nightmare must be lingering in there, I added:

"There's a female up here then, is there? That's a good joke. If the navy ever got wind of it . . . Won't you introduce me to the lady of the house? I wouldn't say no to a little talk with her, you know!"

And I wanted to laugh.

He turned around, bobbing his ghastly death's head up and down.

He was the one singing! . . .

I sprang up as though I'd been punched . . .

Yes, it was old Mathurin Barnabas, the chief keeper of the *Ar-Men*, who was singing in a woman's voice. I don't think the navy suspected that, either.

"What?" I said.

That was all I said, because I was in no mood for singing. Perhaps on dry land I'd have split my sides laughing; but up in a tower where the wind was already whistling like the wail of another damned soul, my heart wasn't in it . . .

He was singing *inside himself*, pursing his thin lips like a Breton piper playing the biniou pipes, imitating their sound.

"O . . . o . . . o . . ."

It came out very softly, so you'd have sworn it wasn't coming from him at all.

I was still looking for the woman, the young, pretty thing in charge of this old reprobate.

Old? He wasn't as old as all that, seen in the full glare of the lamp. Now he was opening the other door of my room and moving toward his lamps with the same dragging, regular step, a watchman's step, the infinitely weary and measured step of those who have been turning in the inner spiral for years on end. A twist of the hip, a twist of the heel; they recall the decks of ancient ships, the roll of their first big fishing boats, and then they go up to the lamp, their eyes already red, weeping blood from having seen the flame dance.

Mathurin couldn't have been fifty. What made him so *ugly* was that he had neither beard nor whiskers; his face was quite naked, the nose turned up so far that it showed the snot, the mouth so dark and winey you'd think he'd just been drinking.

"What in thunder?" I said to myself. "This puzzle needs solving. Where did the old man learn to *sound* like that?"

I got up, shook myself, and fell into step behind him.

Instead of crossing through the lantern room, he plunged out onto the gallery. I followed him; I couldn't retreat, naturally, behind the chief. Except that for him it wasn't difficult to hold on, as he walked almost on all fours. He hung on to the crenellations with his legs just as much as with his arms, and moved like a crab on a rock, perfectly at home.

As for me, I was stifled, first by the song and then by the wind, biting harder and harder.

He checked the knots on the docking crane, and I saw him twist the end of a rope in a mighty grip. No, he was no shrinking damsel, our keeper of the *Ar-Men*! And he'd known worse than the equinoctial gales. Since it didn't hold as firmly as he'd like, he sat astride the parapet and, head down, made a sturdier loop. Then he went into the lantern room, raised a wick on the left, oiled some machinery on the right and, satisfied with his inspection, went out through the door to my bedroom, as he'd come.

I wanted to ask him a question about the regulations. But he wasn't even listening to me. I think he was walking in his sleep, that man, and sleeping like a deaf man!

As he set off down the spiral staircase he hummed his horrible refrain; still his little moaning song, enough to bring the devil to earth, and, on the word *love*, he let out a final owl screech:

"O . . . o . . . o . . . ove . . . ove!"

Which made my hair stand on end.

To get myself back to sleep, I had to make myself say all the worst curses I knew.

III

Two weeks went by, one the very spit of the other, and straight away it was as though I'd been there twenty years; but for those two weeks, I had all the boredom of twenty years to drag along behind me. The first suffering we endure is the one that lasts longest. I was uneasy, sluggish, I began to age. When I listened to the sea battering the foot of the lighthouse, vomiting streams of insults at me, I made out things I'd never heard before.

During the day, everything worked normally: we took breakfast, we smoked a pipe, we polished the furniture or the machinery, we had dinner, we smoked a pipe, and in the evening, we lit the lighthouse's pipe too. Then, as soon as the lamps began to stretch their pink arms out in all directions, the mood changed. If the wind allowed it, we took a little walk around the base, sat for a while on a stone, and waited our turn to be on watch, looking out for the first star; but the stars didn't show themselves, the sky took on a red, coppery tone, the water looked so black it was as though we were moored on tarmac, and giddiness, such a strange giddiness, rose in the chest. It felt as though you were racing along as fast as could be.

Our existence in that place was a preset mechanism: we couldn't forget ourselves for one moment without breaking the clock. We were holding a candle for the ships, and we'd have set light to ourselves, I think, rather than break our word to them. Still, there'd been no warning about the feel of the lighthouse outside of the duty hours. That was something the Brest navy hadn't foreseen, that's for sure. And as for the old man's ways! . . .

The morning after the *concert* he'd treated me to, I looked carefully at the chief, and noticed he had no hair; either he'd tucked it under the earflaps on his woolen cap, or he'd . . . taken it off. I declare! He'd have had to, wouldn't he, since he didn't have a single hair left? That man was completely bald, at least in the morning. Anyway, it wasn't my business. I was half keeper, half servant. My position was hazy. The old man made a point of not saying a word to me. He grunted like a pig or sang like a young girl, but certainly didn't make conversation like a natural man. He disliked me, no doubt about it. Every so often I'd talk to myself, to keep myself company. Back in the State lodgings at the naval training school, some of the comrades weren't very talkative, but we still had a laugh sometimes, and during my voyages I'd exchange comments with my fellow stoker in the hold. Here, nothing . . . silence; except for the roar of the sea, that is.

I told him all about my time on the coasters, stories about China, and plenty of things that had never actually happened; he'd nod, between two mouthfuls of bread, and let out a cluck like a strangled hen, spitting out little bits of crust or lumps of fat, then lose himself in contemplation of the floor.

Once he said to me, out of nowhere:

"Maybe . . ."

And then he added, in a mutter:

"Or maybe not."

At night he changed his tune, quite literally: he climbed up to the lamps whether I was on watch or not, and doubled up on duty with me, not asking me to do anything, not giving me a single order, lolloping about, always with his song on his lips. A nice little

RACHILDE

refrain sung by a damsel dying crushed under the clogs of some filthy scoundrel.

He put on *his hair*, two long tresses which hung down like spaniel's ears, blonde hair, I swear, and he deployed his loveliest piping tones.

I thought:

"He's an old man with funny ways, but that doesn't mean he's lost his touch."

He didn't let anything slip. Up at the top, the lighthouse was kept like a ballroom.

Down below, on the other hand, was none of the navy's business, so it stayed savagely dirty. He did gather up his crumbs of bread with the greatest care (and even the bits he'd spat out, touching them with his fingers, not caring), but he didn't sweep every Sunday, and the worst kind of rubbish was to be found in the corners. His cleanest habit was to answer the call of nature just outside the door, and the smell spread over what we were eating. It made me retch. I cleaned the door, feeling that the sea water crashing against it wasn't enough, and one morning I wound a rag around a broom and cleaned the living quarters, chucking detergent over the whole place. The old man came out of his hole and squinted at me. I showed him the walls with all the grease scrubbed off, the spruced-up door, and the wooden floor swept as clean as the fresh air. He raised one arm, thin as a crab's leg, and traced a few signs on the ceiling, still playing deaf.

We were entitled to shore leave every two weeks; but the method of getting onto the lighthouse made you a bit less eager to see dry land. In stormy weather the crossings were dangerous, sometimes impossible. I wanted to get acclimatized as best I could, and although I did want to stretch my legs, I stayed put on the job for over five weeks. The only distraction I allowed myself was a little cage of canaries. I requested them with a nice polite note delivered to the supply tender, and, at a price, got two superb canaries when the next supplies came. But my rotten luck, you see, was that they were both males; they started to fight endlessly and pluck each other's feathers out as soon as they arrived in my den.

In any case, that wind provided us with all the amusement of a regular battle. Our docking crane broke in the middle, and I had to clamber up the exterior rungs to tie the two pieces together. Splicing them up took me the whole day, with the old man bellowing at me from below, swearing like an angry old shrew, a seagull screeching through the storm. I knew very well that he was more experienced than I was. I'd have liked to see some of that experience, though, battered by gusts of wind, whipped across the back by the rope hanging free, salty spray filling my mouth and eyes, one foot scrunched up between two iron rungs, which were burning hot because I was gripping them so tightly with the agonizingly painful sole of my foot, one arm holding the pole and the other trying to press the links of the chain together. I couldn't see, I couldn't hear, and I felt myself spinning around the light like a bird trying to roast itself once and for all in the flame of the lamps. When the pole was firm in its brackets again, with the newly tarred chain wound in funeral rings around its three injuries, I climbed down, my heart wrecked, my legs done in. Without really realizing how thirsty I was, I thought of the old man's rum. His dessert rum that he'd never offered me, not even a thimbleful! He was sitting at the table. With a box of salted meat on his knee, he was already chewing at his bread, taking no more notice of my appearance than of the bit of chain I'd brought back.

"A beast of a job," I growled.

He nodded.

"Some good hot soup's what I need to get my stomach back to rights . . . but your herrings . . . herrings . . . as though it rained herrings every day, damn it! I can't stand the smell of them!"

I sat down opposite him, but couldn't face breaking open my own bread, which was horribly hard, as usual.

"And never a word to raise a laugh, never asking if I'm happy with the work. You have to admit, chief, you're not an ordinary man."

He remained silent, eyeing the waves, groaning between each mouthful, maybe because it wouldn't go down or because he had toothache.

"We'd be men if we talked like normal people, but we're like prisoners here. I don't know why you sing at night when you're mute from dawn to dusk. Except you're not even mute! You swear when it suits you, when what you should be doing is encouraging me. I may be in prison, but it's the State that's guilty, not me . . . I'm hardly a murderer, am I?"

The old man stood up all of a sudden. He put down his knife and the box of herrings spilled under the table.

"More mess for our manservant to clean up," I murmured, very cross.

Then he spread his arms wide, stretched his crab pincers up to the ceiling, traced all sorts of symbols, over and over like signs of the cross, and went outside with the air of someone who's just remembered something precious.

Remembered something my foot. He was just going to piss in the sea.

"Well, he's cleaning up his act!" I said to myself.

Because usually he did it against the door.

And I fell asleep with my elbows on my bread.

I dreamed of strange things.

First, I saw a beautiful girl coming in from the base, humming. She was holding a knife, the old man's, and she put it ever so gently against the back of my neck. I went cold and turned in my seat, my bread fell to the floor. Automatically, I picked it up. I made all these movements, sleeping or waking, not knowing at all where I was or why I felt completely incapable of moving any further. The young thing had the look of my little Moorish girl, the one whose photograph ornamented my room. She was thin, slim-hipped, tapering down through the legs and ending like a spindle. Her hair, cut short over her forehead, formed a cap like a little urchin. Her hair was brown, her skin yellow gray like an unripe lemon, and she had the glowing eyes of a wild cat, eyes of all different colors, cats' eyes.

"*Like cats!...*"

That phrase was all I could remember of her. I'd known her so little! Going off again straight away on the coaster, leaving her in the charge of four English soldiers quite capable of killing her if she resisted. But ... I knew she wouldn't resist anyone, the blasted little tart ...

And the dream moved away from the lighthouse. I found myself transported to a lush, green island.

It was somewhere near Malta. We were approaching in a sailing boat, an outrigger with its sail attached to the crossbar on the port side. When the wind made the little toy tilt, the sail got wet, and the very end of the leeboard dipped coquettishly into the water. Zuléma, that was the name of my little Moorish girl, had been drinking tafia all night and all morning, and so had I, and the boat took a swallow of water with every breath of wind.

... What a sun! How drunk we were! What a trip, what a swell! Oh! Nothing like the sea's crazy assaults on the lighthouse.

It was happiness cradling us. We were exhausted from all our carousing, but still feasting our eyes on one another, hands and feet intertwined. The sea was so blue it was almost pink where the rudder teased it, and that little skiff was just the shape of a clog, a clog with three sheets to the wind, just like us. She went in such a dead straight line, so purposefully sideways, that it could only end well . . . when all was said and done. Malta? I couldn't see the town and the gardens sloping down alongside the white walls so well anymore. The old fortress was disappearing, collapsing into the new houses, beautiful English houses. Crash! Smash! Everything was falling, one thing on top of another, tumbling into the blue of the sea. There'd be no casualties though, we thought, because we'd had too much to drink that day. It warmed you all over, a real bonfire. My ship, the coaster, decked out with flags and polished to a shine, was purring contentedly at anchor. All the ship's officers, led by the skipper, were gorging themselves at the tables of women from the rich part of town, and as for the rest of us, seamen and lads from the coal bunkers, we brought our little fortunes to the poor parts, scattering our pay packets in all the cabarets in the port.

But it wouldn't be right to say that whenever sailors have a good time it's nothing but a wild binge. That's not true, you see, for there's lots of love in it too. You're the strongest man in the world when you've been good as gold for months, and you don't need to bother drinking much because you're already full to the gills. One more glass offered by a stranger could be the death of you—but the clever ones only drink in women's eyes.

I'd come across Zuléma just as you find a button from a pair of drawers glinting in the mud. You pick it up without really know-ing why . . . and you look at it, stick it in your pocket . . . the next day you look for it, getting an idea all of a sudden, and you notice that the pocket's got a hole . . . someone else will pick up the shiny button, the pretty brass button.

Such a sun! Zuléma was lying on a net left behind by the owner of our clog, wearing her little Moorish costume: a short skirt with billowing pantaloons underneath, and an embroidered jacket over a shirt made of canvas as rough as a sail. She wore her hair cut short like a cap, and her eyes shone . . .

"Like cats!" she said, fluttering her eyelashes.

The boat found the shore all by itself, the keel creaking a little over the sand.

I'd taken her away, this girl, to escape the argy-bargy, wanting to believe for a moment that she was all mine, far from her house with its faded garlands; the girls are free over there, they can follow a man all the live-long day. It's for them that people pray to the Virgin Mary on Sundays.

Zuléma spoke an incomprehensible English patois, but she knew all the filthy words in French, and she admitted later that she was born in Marseille. Her parents had lost her in a street, one evening . . .

"Yes, like cats!"

The island rose up out of the sea, a bouquet held in a bride's hand: orange blossom, lemon blossom, and tamarisk leaves all around, and myrtle leaves, even greener, because the flowers at their center were pale like droplets of milk.

"With cats!"

"Leave me in peace, beast, or we'll never get ashore. Zuléma, you're drunk!"

I wasn't angry, it's just that when I'm tipsy I get coy, and thoughts of God come into my head.

She was wrapping her bare legs around my waist, her head hanging down in the bottom of the boat; she braced her back against the bench, and with her little monkey feet, which were escaping from their gold-threaded slippers, she pinned my arms down ... When I realized that the game was going to last too long, I grabbed her ankles and, not worrying about the rest of her, dragged her ashore. Her head got a ducking, first in the blue water, then in the green weeds; finally, she appeared, her short hair stuck down like a silk cap, in sand the color of corn flour. She lay and dried off there, sneezing and murmuring:

"Oh! Like cats!"

She stayed there, stretched out, her eyelids fluttering, a little bit more sober, at least, and very happy.

I began to gaze at the flowers, and felt more tender:

"There aren't half a lot of them! All those orange trees! All those lemons! What a country! It's like being in church ..."

The little Maltese Moor nodded.

"You see," I said to her, "There is a God! It's as sure as you're a little minx and I'm a poor man. Whether we eat coal or whether we wear a captain's stripes, the flowers were made for everybody, weren't they? We smell them, don't we, just as well as if we had thirty thousand pounds a year?"

She immediately began to jabber on in English, because of those words: *thousand pounds*.

I didn't understand.

We'd already negotiated the price the night before.

She added, in Marseille French:

"And, if you pass by Malta next month, don't forget me ..."

I said *yes* with all my heart. We loved each other, didn't we?

Birds flitted out of the trees and almost brushed our shoulders. I sat down next to her, caressing her small breasts, with no thought of any bad behavior. I was happy because I was like a child with her . . . A really brave lad never gives himself over completely to any woman. Now that I was calm, I didn't want to bite into the apple of her love any more . . . I watched the branches of the orange trees, so pure you could taste the bitterness, and I looked at her mouth, so red, so firmly closed all of a sudden that my own began to water . . .

"I'm sleepy," she said.

She stretched herself out across me, very supple, very nervous, and fell asleep bit by bit, murmuring in her stubborn voice:

"Like cats."

All the while, the sea amused itself by lifting up the boat, giving it a drink by swelling up to its crossbar, and flowers wept down on us like drops of cream.

The sun! . . . Oh sun of little minxes, oh sun of poor men! Cities of love dotted the length of the voyage of our poverty, waystations for our desires, blessed ports of call where our virility anchors itself so tenaciously that it drags corpses up to the surface when we force it away . . .

We'd drunk too much! We hadn't even the strength to drink any more . . . and we'd have to part in the morning . . .

"Up! Stir yourself!" bellowed old Barnabas, in a terrible voice.

I woke with a start. What? Was there a fire on the ship? Were we all summoned on deck?

But no, I wasn't on a ship anymore. No more setting sail! I was on the *Ar-Men* lighthouse, and my principal keeper was standing over me holding his lantern. He'd put on his dog's ears of long blonde hair, the filthy devil, and his death's head of a face was quite pale with fear, or anger. His eyes rolled like a tiger's.

"What, chief?" I stammered, still stiff from my fitful sleep on the table, "The lamp hasn't gone out?"

Because here, lack of light was a serious matter. The old man seized my shoulder in his crab claw and replied in a shriek:

"You never lit it, dog!"

I sprang to the door giving onto the base.

All around us the sea was black as a winding sheet, and here and there we could just make out—like flecks of snow scattered over mountain tops—the foam of the waves.

It was true. We'd forgotten to light the lamp.

IV

In the whole of seafaring memory, it had never happened. No one had ever forgotten to light a lamp, even a third-order one, especially with two keepers in good health and not driven out of their minds by the weather. The wind was blowing hard around Ouessant, but not enough to overturn the cage on top of us, and, despite my dream, nobody had drunk a glass too many.

I didn't linger over all these thoughts. My brain was fogged with visions of girls, and the old man's shout had thrust the idea of our duties into my heart like a narrow blade.

How stupid we were! I didn't dare wonder why he, who was always sticking his nose in, and kept watch when he didn't need to, hadn't lit the lamp himself when the time came.

I climbed up the tower, lamp held high, and arrived sweating, panting, wincing with terror, at the lantern room.

The sky was heavy, tumbling down over your head like a hood. The night, even thicker, sank its velvet claws into your eyes. Down below, the sea rolled, singing its death song and laying out, between one black place and another, its white linen, all ready for dressing sailors one final time.

That strange dizziness, which I'd felt before when I was sitting on the base, made my head spin again. Once again, I felt drawn to the void, sucked down, and had to flatten myself against the gallery parapet to stop myself jumping off into nowhere.

It wasn't the height of the lighthouse or its isolation among the waves that frightened me. I somehow imagined that it was sitting crooked, sloping maybe, because of the misshapen rock it was built on. The rock was certainly lopsided, even if the lighthouse was straight! You can never be certain about the strength of the waves, or the tides. Something can always go wrong in spite of all the engineers' science. Thirty-six years—that's old for something built of stone, slapped furiously by the ocean every day and every night.

I was numb, hanging stupidly onto the grating around the lantern, groping about, trying to open the flue, which I knew like the back of my hand. I felt as though I were still in my dream, sleeping and rocking with the movement of the shadowy waves, one side then the other, caring nothing for reality.

"What? Not lit?... As long as you can have a laugh about it, it doesn't matter! You can't light the lamps from your bed. He's raving, the old madman! Damn and blast him!... Here's my lighter, and there's the first wick ... and after all, lamps revolve all by themselves nowadays!"

That wasn't possible, seeing as the lighthouse had a fixed lamp. It didn't turn. I did though, now toward to sea, now toward the lantern pane. My legs were giving way, I had cramps in my stomach, I thought I felt bats' wings brushing past my eyelids ... Finally, the flame shot up from my feverish fingers, leaped onto the circle of wicks, and a small crackle ran from one part of the mechanism to another. Pink arms of victorious light pushed the darkness back to the edge of the horizon.

I breathed.

No big ships to be seen, no lost fishing boats, an empty sea, almost calm. No danger! We wouldn't be reported to the Brest navy for this affair.

I started dancing for joy.

It overflowed from my chest to my lips. I sang, I shouted, I stamped my heels on the flagstones of the gallery. I wasn't hungry or thirsty anymore. I was lifted higher than the *Ar-Men* lighthouse. I was swimming in the banks of heavy clouds that were turning copper now, then pink, and laughing, just like me.

Ah, the old wolf! What a fright he'd given me! I didn't go down again, but went to my room, letting the bright light in, and I sat myself down at my table to record the error, very faithfully.

But then I was seized by doubts again.

Admitting to this mistake, which hadn't led to any disaster, might make my employers judge me too harshly. The old man should have acted like a good skipper and companion, and given me a tap on the shoulder. After all that sweating and slaving I'd done on the perishing hoist, I'd had some kind of blackout. My teeth chattered at the memory. All the while, the old man had strolled up and down the base, smoking his pipe. I could mention that. I twisted my pen in my fingers. Writing wasn't my strong suit. I thought about a lot of useless things. One hour more, one hour less, who cared? ... Still, my shirt stuck to me when I thought of all the boats counting on us just as much as they did on Our Lord.

We didn't often see big ships. They seldom paid us a call, what with the long stretch of reefs just under the surface. We caught glimpses of them on clear days, and it was like seeing a darker line of waves, a path traced through the huge prairie, the prairie whose grass was the hair of the drowned.

We had a so-called lifeboat to go out and look at them, but the water crashed onto the back of the *Baleine* reef so hard, it damped your curiosity right down.

Best to give it a try around midday, when the sky was clear.

We'd wait a bit, we'd see . . .

I heard the chief humming in his *woman's* voice.

He was climbing up to the top, as he always did around ten o'clock in the evening, his lantern swinging at the end of his crab claw. He'd forgotten our escapade. An isolated escapade, yes, thanks to him.

That song, mocking my distress, enraged me. I began to write with my most valiant stoker-mechanic handwriting . . . that the assistant keeper, *as yet little accustomed to his profession*, and following a serious indisposition, had forgotten . . .

There! Now it was as though the notary had declared it.

They're gospels, logbooks are.

As he came into my room, the old man looked at me with his shining gaze, the dirty owl! He looked over my shoulder and began to snigger:

"Papers?" he mumbled. "That won't stop the wind blowing!"

I crossed out the word "serious," just to show off a bit.

He examined the logbook, and seemed dazzled, perhaps by the glare of the lamps. They were shining bright that evening, I can vouch for that.

"Boy," he said, his voice suddenly low, "I don't know how to read any more."

He spoke regretfully, like someone at confession.

How the devil can someone manage to forget how to read?

I got up, setting down my pen, rather proud of my mission, the mission for the Brest navy: *to replace the intelligence of an old man in decline.* Perhaps they knew things about him that I didn't. He was a crafty fox when it came to the work, this old man, but he had no schooling, couldn't keep his accounts himself. I'd never seen him writing, it was true. I only remembered one nasty little ha'penny book that he'd take out in the evening, just so he could fall asleep on it while he waited for his turn on watch. He couldn't read my handwriting, most likely.

"I was told to record the squalls," I answered, strutting about a little. "It'll save you a job ... and, in exchange, you really should have woken me earlier, skipper!"

He was still looking at me, his gaze becoming gradually more distant, wandering, searching for ideas in the corners of my room.

He traced a few lines in the air, growled some outlandish words, and left, dragging his leg and swinging his elbows.

"Oh, no hard feelings, Monsieur Barnabas."

He turned abruptly:

"Don't slip up too many times, sonny! I can tell tales on you too."

If he hadn't been so old, I'd have given him a kicking.

He started up his song, and I finally understood a few words of his diabolical refrain:

> *It was the tower, beware,*
> *It was the tower ... of love!*
> *Of love ... o ... o ... ve!*

My God, which tower of love was he on about, the poor wretch? We were both living in a tower where we had to beware, but it wasn't because of love, and anyway, maidens to marry were in short supply here.

The night passed peacefully, and the next morning I woke up as my canaries were having their wash, splashing each other with a quarter of my water ration.

The horrible little creatures upset me with all their fighting. There was *Cadic* and *Cadichet*. *Cadic*, the older one, must have had gout. He flew awkwardly, always folding one leg under his chest;

Cadichet was more alert and greedier, always eating and spreading his portion of millet all over the room to annoy his companion. The older one sometimes sang so piercingly it was enough to burst my eardrums. The younger let out little sparrow-like chirps.

I wanted a family, a little brood, pretty little chicks, well-trained, carefully crossbred, with a good repertoire of trills, and I especially wanted a green mule bird, so I could put him in a separate cage and teach him proper songs. Instead of all that, I was falling victim to two nasty birds locked in endless quarrel, dirtying my room and wasting drinking water as though it flowed from taps here.

I'd paid a hundred *sous* for them. Not a good investment, upon my word! I couldn't let them fly away through the window seven miles from dry land. I couldn't let them die of hunger, and it would be impossible to persuade the supply boat to take them back. I was reluctant to kill them. I'd been on the lighthouse for six weeks, not taking my days off, but I couldn't hope for an extra leave just so I could go and exchange a male canary for a female.

What was worse, my mistake of the day before wouldn't inspire generosity in my employers, and old Barnabas wouldn't allow me, after such a short time, a visit to the . . . birds of Brest.

I was full of melancholy.

My room, in the dawn light, didn't inspire mad gaiety either. It was bright, bare as an eggshell, and seemed destined to remain empty forever. My camp bed, very clean with polished legs, was like a hospital bed. It took up as little space as possible, and my little keeper's clock glinted on the shelves like a set of surgeon's tools. The books lying on my table didn't tempt me. I'd never been a great reader. When it came to my work or even just my own common sense, I preferred to come up with my own ideas to learning about other people's.

What I needed now, to light up my brain, was a few animals capering around my legs. I thought of a monkey or a dog:

"Why not get married, have children? Find a nice little fisherman's daughter, born and bred in *Sein*, where the women are beautiful, they say. Let her manage the bit of land, a cow, chickens, and go and surprise her in her little house every fortnight. After a year I'd be a principal keeper, sure as could be, with double pay and a week off every month on dry, God-fearing land. Good, Breton-speaking Breton women know what hard work is, and never complain about the wind blowing. It's an honor for them to be the wife of a principal keeper, on the coast or the islands."

I got to thinking about all sorts of things, listening to my canaries quarrelling like two young men, fed up and angry enough to kill one another. There was me dreaming of marriage! Me, Jean, the poor deprived wretch. While I got washed, not wasting any fresh water, I reflected that I was a good lad, in body and heart, with a gentle character, not too inclined to drink, not argumentative, never moaning, and often able to understand things beyond my education. I didn't *boast* much in life, but when you're born without a silver spoon in your mouth, you've a right to feel a little proud.

I wasn't bad, physically, a little thin perhaps, but I had good brown eyes, white teeth, brown hair, all the usual things, you know, and if I was a bit over-inclined to the other sex, it was only because pretty girls would have me cheaper than my comrades, proof that they could see my worth when it came to the sentimental side of things.

Yes indeed, the woman question needed an answer, and soon, because . . . well . . . it was getting worse!

"*No women!*" That was what the brocaded Captain had insisted.

A marriage set you up for life . . . so . . .

What about the old man? Was it because he'd lost his wife that he stopped wanting to leave his owl's nest?

Through the little window in my lookout room, a very thick oval pane with a steel net over it, you could see the great, heaving sea, rolling enough to make your stomach churn. It was like being up in a balloon, with nothing to help you get your bearings. We were suspended in the void that gaped below us, gaped as though to swallow us better, and sometimes a terrible vertigo would rise up, grasp our throats, and shake us from head to foot. We didn't walk, we turned with the sea, and when the wind whipped the water to tremendous heights, it seemed to lift the lighthouse too; we felt it vibrating from top to bottom, swaying, waving, waltzing . . . never had a doomed ship performed a dance like this. It was the eternal dance, the torment of those who have traveled too much down in the hold. Afterward, everything was still again, but the brain set sail, leaped onwards, lost itself in unknown places . . . the race to madness.

I gazed at the immense emptiness, wracked with sadness. Over there, toward the *Basses froides*, a dark spot, a sail, then another: fishing boats attempting the difficult passage, on the hunt for merchandise to sell at the next fish market. Four o'clock in the morning! They struggle, flounder against one another, form a line, form two groups, and off they go, sails tight as drums, like pigeons who've spotted a glint of wheat underneath the green of the grass.

Up we get. We've work to do as well.

My lamps are clean, my oil cups are filling, the mechanism's working honorably. The weather's quite stable, no danger of the glass smashing today. I should be satisfied.

And I don't know why, but I'm worried. I yawn nervously. I'm hungry . . . I need to go down.

I met the old wolf down on the base.

"Nice weather, Captain," I said to him, as politely as I could.

He gave his usual grunt, waving his right hand like an octopus. I inspected our domain, clambering up the outside rungs and sticking my nose into all the holes where you could touch the rock. I got blasted by spray and had enough salty slaps to set me sneezing for an hour. It smelled of the tide, of rot, of fish guts and plenty of other unmentionable things.

I gathered some mussels, so big that half a dozen were enough for my breakfast. It made a change, at least, something more appetizing than the endless kippers, but as I was climbing back up to offer some to the chief, wanting to show my goodwill that morning, he made a strange gesture and turned his face away.

"Poison!" he snarled, nastily.

"What? Poison, in mussels? You must be joking!"

The lighthouse couldn't be built on a copper frame, and there surely wasn't any rotting algae lurking in the holes in the rock, because the water didn't carry any out to these distant spots.

What a character the old man was!

I sucked greedily on the shell I'd just opened with the knife on my belt. It was beautifully fresh. Oh, sweet Saint Barnabas, I remember how fresh it was. It was a virgin's eye, dark blue swimming in pearly albumen, so transparent, so smooth . . . a lovely mussel!

Still, it had a strange, insipid little aftertaste. It stayed in your gullet, like a taste of mud, or . . . but why wouldn't these rock mussels have been clean?

It would've been a different story if I'd got them off one of the quays in Brest where they chuck diseased cat corpses.

After I'd done my morning cleaning and scoured the sardine tins that the old man used to pile up on either side of the fireplace, I hurried to collect another batch of mussels. The holes in the rocks bristled with them around midday, as the tide rose and swelled over the lower part of the tower. You could only get around the foot of the lighthouse in a boat. I untied the lifeboat, which was ready to launch, as the rules demanded. It was an old, patched-up rowing boat, poorly built and incapable of riding the swell. I hauled it along by brute force, sticking close to the wall, hanging on to an old iron rail. These precautions weren't excessive: the current was too much for any ordinary maneuvers.

This particular current came straight from the *Bay of the Dead*. The lighthouse was in the middle of an eddy formed by the *Sein* strait and the last few islands and islets of the huge embankment. On maps, the tower looked like a little man standing in the bottom of a bowl, and everybody knows that when water washes around a fixed point, it collects all kinds of things.

The whole lot washes around the pair of enormous bridge piers formed by the two tails of Brittany and Cornwall. With every tide, the immense stampede of water from the Atlantic arrives at this inlet, between these two piers, and forms a furious river, which for six hours, throws itself into the North Sea for six hours, then goes back toward the Ocean for the next six hours.

That pretty little river is the *Channel*.

When we were training, they'd tell us about the frequent shipwrecks, boats lost almost every day near the *Tévennec* and *Vieille* lighthouses, and the *Sein* strait, but we were philosophical about it.

"We're all mortal!"

But we never gave a thought to what happens to all the drowned who aren't brought back by the waves within the traditional nine days. (Nine days! That's the lying-in period for this great expeller of men.)

They're eaten by fish.

Ha! Not all of them! There are some places where fish don't go: the current breaks up their shoal, and they scatter.

The monsters of the seabed don't come up around the rocks, and the flesh-eaters from the surface don't stay in the warm foam to be whisked up in the air by the whip of the rip currents.

You never saw Mathurin Barnabas fishing on the base.

I disturbed an enormous crab, which beat a leisurely retreat, deeper into the black hole where it resided; other slimy creatures, and a lamprey eel, crept and zigzagged along the stonework.

I collected a pile of mussels in my cap.

I was tied firmly, with one foot on the edge of my boat and my boot almost completely inside the hole in the rock. The giant shadow of the lighthouse loomed above, forming a path leading to this mysterious cave. The huge waves were, for the moment, respectful of this sad corner of the world, leaving the desolate place in relative calm. Not a blade of grass, not a scrap of algae, not a tuft of lichen, not a shard of white or pink shell, no color, no reflections: everything was black, an intense black, so intense it seemed to shine; the water harbored an inner flame, a dark fire purer than jet. At the very center of this mourning, a strange object could be seen. It looked like a piece of wood, a fragment of bulrush paler at one end. A creature? No. It was only revolving because the water was circulating around the rock.

This current came from far away, furious at first, then more furtive, crouching under the waves and herding all sorts of flotsam in front of it, like a flock of sheep.

It had brought this ... dropping the rest along the way. This was flotsam too, tiny human flotsam. It looked like a miniature snake, a reddish snake whose tapered head seemed translucent, made of porcelain ...

It was a finger.

It went along all by itself. My god, yes! You get separated from your brothers, one stormy old day, by the teeth of a conger eel or because the *hand*, as it floated up from the bottom, rots away as it grasps the lifesaving plank.

Very often, fingers are cut at the knuckle that wears a ring. The swollen flesh tears, and the ring, a worn wedding band, serves as a knife, gradually sawing the little soft bone already broken by the final struggle, and the liberated finger makes off, straight as an arrow, pointing the way to nothingness.

Anyway, I don't know why it was there, the poor thing, but it was definitely *a finger*.

I hurled the contents of my cap full of mussels back into the sea, and rushed back into the lighthouse, clutching my belly ... I was sick for two days! ...

V

Bent over his little book, the old man didn't hear me coming up the spiral staircase, and carried on reading most devoutly.

He was mouthing the words:

"A . . . a . . . a . . . apple! B . . . b . . . b . . . boat!"

And he stopped, quavering, his cheeks puffed out in concentration. The ceiling lamp shone directly over him.

He wasn't a reassuring sight, for all his pious reading, that blasted old Barnabas.

The cap pulled down over his forehead, with two blonde dog's ears hanging from it, made his face more pallid, more naked than a monkey's behind. His protruding cheekbones had the waxy yellow shine of church candles, and his eyes rolled green and glassy like those of a dead fish. His horrible woolen clothes, never taken off, never brushed, looked as though they'd been coated in tobacco juice for the whole ten years of their existence. (I already knew that he wore his boots to bed.) You never saw any linen on him, either dirty or clean, and it was safe to assume that he didn't know what shirts were for, because he used to gaze at me and whistle when he saw me washing mine. He was beyond dirty, beyond ugly—he was shame made man.

I went up behind him and tried to make out what it was that he read so diligently every evening. There were plenty of books on the shelf, the ragbag ordered by the navy by way of amusing the prisoners of the sea: science books, travel tales, and nice tame love stories: *Robinson Crusoe, Paul and Virginie, Fontaine's Fables.* But his little book looked more like a catechism or even a . . .

I straightened up, and a shiver ran down my spine.

I'd seen it all right.

It was an ABC.

Old Barnabas, principal keeper of the *Ar-Men* lighthouse, who'd studied and got his diploma long ago, was reading . . . the ABC, so he mustn't know how to read! . . .

Why did that make my skin crawl, instead of making me laugh?

I stood mute with horror.

"What is it, Maleux?" he said, lifting his pug-nose to me. "You got the runs?"

Because of the business with the mussels, he was reminding me of my sensitive stomach.

I was still gazing at the little book. I replied very respectfully—it wasn't often that he deigned to speak to me:

"Skipper, the wind's rising up there. We'll have complications tonight, I fear. So . . ."

"Watch together then!" he grunted, not troubling himself to say anything else, and went back to his reading, halting painfully over the vowels:

"A . . . a . . . a . . . I . . . u . . . aou . . . aou!"

People who live safe and warm in their quarters on dry land can't imagine what it is to spend an evening at sea on a ship that doesn't move, where there's no hope of landing anywhere and you never stop hearing the wind.

That night it made such a racket, the wind, it made you want to die. Seagulls' screams, women's screams, witches' screams, devils' screams, they were all mixed up in it. The note was constantly changing, and what had been a distant wail would come up close the next minute and laugh and spit on our door. The door held firm, but spray spurted underneath. The base, flagstones, and steps were doused with water, so much so that you could *feel yourself leaning*. The music of it all filtered down the spiral staircase from up top, even though I'd closed the door to the gallery. Torrents of shouting and swearing were amplified as they came down this great factory chimney, crashing down on our shoulders like the rage of the ocean itself.

The old man read aloud haltingly, very peaceful.

Strange as it seems, that horrified me more than anything else!

I stood lingering near the table, not choosing to read alongside him. The alphabet wasn't to my taste, and I didn't want to let my guard down. Why? I don't really know. I only remember that I never once took my eyes off him.

"The lamps are working well. I found three big swifts on the lantern frame, but they hadn't broken the glass ... we'll have to see ..." I said, mechanically.

"We'll have to see!" the old man repeated, spelling aloud with all his might.

I wanted to go and watch up on top. But I hesitated. Had my stay on the lighthouse made me afraid?

In any case, I had no willpower, no strength, no sensible ideas.

I sat on the table, letting my legs hang down soft like cotton wool.

A mist hung around us—smoke from the oil and a damp cloud curling under the door with the plumes of spray.

The clock swept the hours away at its monotonous pace amid the pandemonium, and when the rock itself creaked, the clock creaked too like an old deaf woman shifting her chair and coughing.

Ah! We made a pretty couple, the old man and I!

We were galley slaves sitting on the same bench, attached to the same chain, but we didn't know each other, didn't understand each other. The things we said to one another had no human meaning. We ate the same bread, drank the same cider, and didn't share the rum of friendship: we each guarded it jealously for ourselves (because I'd bought some good tafia too, so as to cure my bellyache from the mussels).

I thought about the comrade who'd *died in an accident*, perished of boredom, perhaps, on an evening like this, after five or six years of . . . service. While he was adjusting the docking crane or mending the lantern frame one stormy night, he must've fallen from up there and bounced off the gangway, his head smashed . . . unless . . .

"Tell me, shipmate," I murmured, doing my best to sound idiotic, "Is it interesting, the book you're reading?"

The old man looked up.

"It's a fine book," he answered, "but once you lose the thread, it's hard to find it again."

"You've lost the thread of . . . (I was going to say the alphabet, but I bit my tongue) of your story?"

"Yes, Maleux, I lost it . . . one stormy night."

He sighed and added:

"He was a good lad, even so!"

I was taken aback, because we'd both come up against the idea of the dead man, my predecessor.

"What? So did you know how to read . . . other things, when he lived here, that lad?"

"I read . . . his soul, and now the devil can keep him instead of me!"

The old man set down his book and raised his hand, making a sign toward the ceiling.

His eyes seemed cloudier than usual. He wasn't losing the thread of ... the alphabet, that old-timer.

"Hon! ... on ... or .. r!" he crooned, all of a sudden.

And he added:

"I'm from Ouessant, born and bred, and for twenty years I've been the keeper of the Tower of ... love, of the *Ar-Men*."

He took off his cap as if in salute.

"All right, all right!" I stammered, seized with horror. "I didn't want to offend you, Monsieur Barnabas. Just trying some chit-chat, to pass the time while things are bad. Anyway, I'm not nosy. I've no interest in mixing myself up in other people's affairs."

I should have had a terrible urge to laugh because, when he lifted his cap, the old man had lifted his hair off too, but his head, white and shining like a moon, had an extraordinary effect on me.

He fixed his dead-fish eyes on mine, paralyzing me.

"What's got into you, Maleux, to go tittle-tattling about me?"

I decided to tease him.

"Now now, father Barnabas, I'm not telling tales on anyone here. It's the *wind madness* that's getting to you."

Wind madness is a well-known affliction among lighthouse keepers, especially new ones. You end up hearing something calling your name up and down the stairs, along the ladders—anywhere you can whistle.

"Yes," he said, in a melancholy voice, like a querulous old woman, "I've got the madness. Still, there's no one my equal in the profession; I never take leave, I don't drink, I don't talk, and I hardly sleep anymore; you'll not find my equal on all the lights of the coast, and you can tell that to our officers."

"I think they know it, Monsieur Barnabas. They sang your praises to me six months ago, when I came here. No, there's none like you, and it's not your fault if the lad fell . . . the same could happen to me tomorrow. We're all at the mercy of him that blows."

He seemed to think for a minute, then he sniggered, stroking the blonde hair that adorned his greasy cap.

"It's my belief that won't happen to you, Maleux."

"God knows! God willing!"

"God . . . He's dead," he replied harshly, and he turned his back on me.

"Are you going up, Captain?"

"Yes, it's my time . . . I can tell it's getting worse up there . . . Don't need you."

I stayed there quite still, perched on the table, opposite the cap that he'd forgotten to put back on.

It's the tower, beware!
It's the tower of love . . . o . . . o . . . ove!

The voice rose, mingled with the wind, and grew distant, like the voice of a girl being strangled on the dunes one night of equinox storms.

I gazed at the hat. After a while I picked it up gingerly, amazed at how greasy it was: like seal skin.

On both sides, hanging down from the earflaps, were blonde locks of hair, beautiful locks that shone like silk. It was young hair for sure, and the very finest.

As I turned the hair over and over, I saw that it was attached to the leather earflaps by some kind of softer, paler skin, and that this skin was sewn onto the leather with coarse string.

"There's a strange invention! Where the devil did the old man find these ornaments?"

I lifted the hair a little, moving it away from the almost transparent skin, like parchment, and . . .

An appalling crash reverberated through the lighthouse, shaking it from base to tip. I heard the old man bellowing my name from up above.

"The cage has smashed!" I cried out. "We're bloody well done for!"

I threw the cap down any old how and leaped up the spiral staircase.

The cage wasn't smashed, but half open on the north side. A jet of water, the final slap of the wind, or, perhaps, a bird-stone, had broken through the glass and destroyed one of the regulators. The lights were fizzling out, turning black and stinking like torches, and an acrid, choking smoke, darker than night, was pouring out onto the gallery and blinding us so we couldn't even see our hands.

"Take hold of this!" said the chief. He'd thrust one arm inside the broken glass, tearing his skin in the process, and he was holding up the weight of the machinery all by himself.

I took his place while he tried to relight the wicks, sprinkling burning petrol on them. There was no risk of fire at this height, and in any case our orders were to set everything on fire rather than let the light go out.

"Hold on to it! Now . . . heave! Hold tight to the end! Hold tight! . . ." bellowed the chief, in the great clamor of the wind.

It took three hours to repair that mechanism.

The wicks went out in spite of our streams of petrol, and the sea spray landed on them like strips of wet cloth, stopping up the light and stopping up our eyes. Birds (it seemed to me that wings were brushing my face) whirled about in the smoke, making it thicker still and whipping us with their barbed feathers. I could barely hold what I needed to hold. Everything was being pulled upward from somewhere high in the sky, and the more I swore at the demons of the air to let go, the more of them came to the aid of their comrades.

While we fought bravely, the old man's head shining white in the chaos, just like the sphere of the moon, there was a brief respite . . . oh, just enough time to say an *Ave* and take a breath, when we both turned cold, a deathly cold: *a bell was ringing to the north*.

"Ship!" shouted the old man.

A ship, near to us, near enough to hear the bell. Shipwreck was inevitable.

All day there'd been mist so thick you couldn't see your right arm. Freezing jets of spray and avalanches of rain mixed with hail so it seemed the clouds were crumbling into pieces! The sea rearing up to the first floor of the lighthouse, lashing it with its salt whips—we even ate a huge fish that dropped onto our doorstep. After that gift, the water was taking its revenge and bringing us human souls! . . .

That sound of the bell ringing, clear and sharp as vinegar, in that endless thunderous racket, felt like a needle prick. You couldn't see anything by leaning over the gallery parapet—no masthead light and no stern light, and we could only guess that the lights of this ship would never be lit again.

"Perhaps we should get the lifebelts and the boat ready," I said to the old man, my teeth chattering.

"No use," he said calmly, tying his handkerchief around his hairless head, because he was horribly hot in the cold wind. "They'll wreck on the promontory . . . might as well be dead already."

"Oh! The poor devils! We can't just sit and wait here, calmly . . . they're men . . ."

"So are we!"

I could see there was nothing more to be done. The little lifeboat was just for show, good for nothing but mussel fishing along the rock. We couldn't go to their aid without passing over the back of the *Baleine* reef. So, as nobody in a boat goes over a reef without leaving his body and soul there . . . we had to suffer their loss. We'd risked being carried off by the wind to keep our light on, and our duty ended there.

The bell was still ringing.

We went back down to fetch some rope and steel rods and climbed up again in silence (the old man even forgetting his little love song) to finish our job properly.

By the time we'd climbed up . . . the ringing had stopped!

Once, when the squalls let up for a few seconds, I turned to the north and heard voices shouting. These weren't the cries of the demons of the air.

The old man didn't even take off his cap, which he'd put back on over his knotted handkerchief when he went downstairs.

He said, twisting the rod around the light with a vigorous hand:

"That's it!"

I'm not devout, only the night was so dark, the wind so terrible . . . I crossed myself.

The old man looked at me, then his eyes slid to the side:

"What's all that for?" he said, crossly. "God's dead!"

VI

No one can possibly imagine what rain is like on a lighthouse out at sea. It blurs everything, it wets everything, it melts your brain and dissolves your bones; you drip away bit by bit, watery like a cloud, and you'd jump at any excuse to go and be part of the water yourself, the great final water.

It had been raining for a week.

No more squalls, no more moaning: just a quiet, interminable *hou hou*, like a little old woman on her deathbed, and the sound of the rain, a sound of tiny feet pitter-pattering but never moving.

For three miles all around it was like gray wool, carded here and there by the crests of the waves. Sky and sea blended to produce a single tableau of boredom.

I'd made plans to go for a jaunt in Brest, or over to *Sein*, to try my hand at finding a fiancée and calm my nerves! But as my day's leave fell after the business with the wreck, I didn't dare go or ask for a substitute.

My marriage plans were on the rocks, and so was I; they slipped into the water with the clouds, and the ocean drank me up, along with big ships, little canaries, and all men . . .

We did have one distraction, though. At high tide, the old man would settle himself on the edge of the lowest step of the base, harpoon in hand. When we'd reported the catastrophe to the supply boat, we'd heard back, through the megaphone:

"English ship. *Dermond-Nestle*, coming back from the headland. Watch for wreckage!"

And we fished for wreckage. But there wasn't much, yet. Barrels and planks, a few copper machine parts. Along the whole stretch of the coast, on the edge of every reef, there were men, young and old, harpoons at the ready. And the navy was sending messages down the lines wherever the sea might serve up something useful.

A fine life!

As for me, I carried out my duties on weaker and weaker legs, exasperated deep inside but lacking any energy to take myself in hand.

One morning, when the canaries were tearing each other to pieces in their cage, my patience ran out. I grabbed them in a fit of anger and threw them out into the void so they could find out if the grass was greener there. The two little yellow balls of fluff became grey as they plummeted through the fog, then twirled a couple of times, and were swallowed by a wave.

Bye bye birds!

Now I'd get myself a monkey, a dog, or . . . a woman.

The old man didn't say much, just sat there with his harpoon poised, as usual, but his rotten-fish eyes lit up when he looked at the fatal spot. He gazed at the back of the *Baleine*, the long blackish expanse to the north that the water never covered completely; it was from there that the gifts for the navy would arrive. He lay in wait from dawn.

A fine profession!

We might not be able to save the poor seafarers, but we could collect the planks. It wasn't easy, mind you. All the wreckage revolved as it floated along and unless it collided with the foot of the lighthouse, we had no chance of seeing it again. Some pieces would execute a dive, disappearing mysteriously into the *cellar* of the rock and never coming up again, making food for our mussels.

One evening, I came out to watch alongside my old comrade. We smoked our pipes in the rain, not sharing our thoughts because we hadn't any new ones. He was thinking over his alphabet, most likely; I was counting the days to get through before the next leave from that purgatory. Water from the sky ran down our backs and over our boots, soaking our clothes as though they were sponges; we swallowed pints of it in spite of ourselves, just by sucking our pipe stems, and the blue smoke turned to grey fog. We were smoking rain, more or less!

The lighthouse lamp was like new, brought to life by a big stock of oil, but it was transformed into a sort of yellow, sulfurous vapor, like the lights of trains when they're in a tunnel with their plumes of smoke billowing around them. The waves foaming in this diffuse light were the color of asphalt, and it was no joke.

Even less amusing was the bit of wreckage that came to us, carried from inky swell to inky swell, pallid in that cursed twilight.

"A head! Chief . . . there, next to the *Baleine* . . . A drowned man, chief!"

"Let it come!" he replied, calmly.

I felt the rainwater running faster down my back.

It was a man. Almost sitting up on the sea, a lifebelt keeping him afloat. He was in his shirtsleeves, chest puffed up big enough to burst, head thrown back, hair stuck down, dead eyes still looking searchingly at something far away, mouth wide open, still emitting the shout that had fallen silent . . . He'd been a goner for a week, that one, because he had patches of mold on his skin like something stuffed.

He passed by, revolved once, swayed a little, saluted us most politely, and, neatly avoiding our harpoon, slipped away, full speed ahead.

"They're past their best!" murmured Barnabas, refilling his pipe.

"Oh Chief! It's too much!"

I was trembling with horror. And he dared joke. I certainly couldn't. I'd have liked to say a mass for him. At the *Tévennec* lighthouse they had a chapel, at least. Here we were more alone than anywhere else in the world.

Then a barrel came along, but it split against the flagstone and fell apart.

Next came some ropes, a lump of mast, tins of food. We took one with some English words on it.

It was green beans (I happened to know those words).

Then another drowned man: this one was a sailor stretched out fully clothed on a table, his head buried in his arms. You'd have sworn he was asleep.

I went inside for a moment to record the . . . passersby. When I came back to join the old man I gave a cry of horror. There was a whole gang of them going by, all bound up together in a raft of corpses, lots of young men, a sort of school outing, all dressed the same, jostling, twirling around, a crowd of swimmers heading for land, eager for home.

The last one trailed his head at the end of a red rope coming out of his neck.

I stood frozen to the spot, a lump in my throat, harpoon in hand.

"But what can we do, for God's sake, what can we do?" I kept on repeating, not knowing what I was saying.

"Nothing! They've all come up from the bottom, except the one with the belt," the old man replied philosophically.

Oh, he'd seen a good few shipwrecks, he had! He knew how things were done, from the bottom to the surface, and the land of corpses held no secrets for him, the monster.

A monster! No. He did his duty, steadfast at his post when the storm was blowing. He still carried the scars of serious injuries from defending the lantern up there from the fury of the wind. He didn't balk at the work. He drank little, barely slept any more, and never asked for leave. An old madman, but a solid fellow all the same.

Still, my stomach turned over to hear him explaining those things in that voice of his, like an old woman in her second childhood; he was talking now, chattering like a magpie:

"Lifebelts? Oh, they all have them, all the better to feel themselves dying! When you sink straight down, it's over straight away, but lifebelts are little teases. With them, they hope, they shout, they float about ... but they're never saved. Three years ago, I saw one passing near the reef tip one day, still moving. He wriggled so much he turned himself upside down, with his legs waving in the air. They're so stupid, drowning people! When they stop along the *Baleine*, they go green in the sun until the next high tide. The water takes them back, rolls them about, and then they go down to *look for* the best currents. They're coming out in force now, this next batch. It's lots of rich people, first-class passengers; the sailors cosseted them until the very last moment; they all got their pretty burial ring ... to ensure they have a pleasant voyage. The sailors are freer once the toffs are taking a dip. You've seen proof ... We've only seen one, haven't we? And I bet we won't see any more sailors, at least not this evening."

"So you think it'll be long, this procession past our front door? Good God!"

"Yes, my young lad, it makes you sick," sniggered the old man, his sinister eyes glowing green, "But this is just the beginning. I don't collect dead bodies. You can go to bed if your guts are growling. I can't promise I'll save all the survivors, seeing as there aren't any around here. I'll pick up … (and here he hesitated) … anything preserved! There you go, here comes a bottle."

I'd turned cold. I couldn't raise a laugh. I threw my harpoon down on the stones:

"Chief," I said to him, very solemnly. "You've got no soul. You should watch out! Two good Christians, marooned at sea, as we are here, shouldn't laugh about a tragedy like this. We aren't devout, I admit that, but to be joking when torrents of bodies are floating past, that I can't take. I could easily skedaddle, you know."

"Go on then, bugger off! I didn't come looking for you. Still trying to tell tales on me, are you? D'you think I don't know why you're here? …" He was shouting now, suddenly furious. "They told you to keep an eye on me, didn't they? But I'm not such a fool as they think. You've slipped up too. Let the light go out up there, on an evening when you were *certainly* on watch … all those filthy corpses out there could easily have been on your conscience, d'you hear me, Maleux. Is that clear? Is it?"

I recoiled as though he'd hit me full in the face. What he said was true; and what if the wreck had happened on the day of my mistake! … Because there was no getting around it, that mistake, it was clear as day—I'd had to record it myself in the logbook.

"Chief, it's true I made a mistake … but … I've got my conscience. I'm no murderer."

All the corpses were swirling around me now, making me dizzy. They didn't float away, and I could still see them, some with their mouths open wide in a final cry, other with their eyes fixed forever on the last star they'd ever see. On they went, in a great flock, in rows, two by two, six together, one all alone, small as a child, and they looked like an enormous wedding party spread out for the last dance of the night.

"No," I repeated dully, "No, I'm no murderer, Monsieur Mathurin Barnabas!"

"So what? Nor am I!" he replied, turning his head at the sight of a cask caught on the edge of the second step.

He harpooned the cask.

I climbed back up to the lighthouse, my legs giving way, my eyes lowered.

I'd seen enough to last me my whole life!

My dinner was short. I broke up a bit of biscuit and climbed back up to the gallery.

Up there the air seemed clearer.

In my room, I inspected a little mechanism that I needed to polish up. I oiled the cups to make sure the regulators would run smoothly, and when my work was done, I sat down to read whatever came to hand, trying not to think about the macabre parade outside.

But one idea kept clawing at my mind.

Why the devil hadn't we seen a single woman float by?

At first this idea comforted me a little. I was reading *Paul and Virginie*, a lovely story where the woman is also drowned toward the end. And I remembered the lady's long blonde hair (or was it brown? I can't really remember) stretched on the sand of the seashore when Paul . . . Yes, that was why there were no women. Because we save women first, according to true French manners, and they travel less than men. They stay at home in the warmth, with their children hiding in their skirts.

The book dropped from my hands.

And all of them waiting for their men on the jetties, over there!

I wouldn't have minded comforting one of them.

Oh, to have a sweet woman, a loving one, waiting for you, her pink mouth ready for a kiss on your return . . .

"Like cats!"

And the old memory of the Moorish girl came back to me.

I'd seen her again on my second voyage to Malta, but she wasn't free, and she only gave me her photograph. The photograph I'd kept so devotedly, even though it had been ruined by the Marseilles flies.

Oh, women!

I fell asleep, seeing things and sighing, and I had a strange dream.

I dreamed that a drowned woman . . . who had the old man's hair, the way he wore it in the evening . . .

Habit woke me just in time for my shift. I got up with difficulty.

"A foul dream," I said to myself, ashamed of the whole thing.

. . . But it had come in spite of me . . . and really, in the *Ar-Men* lighthouse it couldn't happen any other way . . .

"It's the tower of Love!" I sniggered to myself, wanting to make fun of my own weakness.

Lost in my thoughts about living in the *Tower of Love*, I suddenly realized I hadn't heard the boss's usual refrain. Was he going to spend the whole night there at the bottom of steps, harpoon at the ready?

I did my round of the lamps and cleaned the glass, filthy with slimy water from the endless rain. From deep within the cave of rocks there rose a low roar: the water was letting out its hollow moan, thrashing about in violent rage at its own powerlessness to demolish us . . . The sea is delightful! Suddenly a new song began to rise, not spiraling up through the interior but coming from *outside*, from the waves. The old man was singing his song, off toward the *Baleine*, abeam the lighthouse, and he was *moving away* . . .

I stood there for a moment, stunned, wondering if I wasn't losing my mind! Why, seeing all those carcasses going past in one evening was enough to drive anyone a bit mad. The old man was going away, leaving the lighthouse, peacefully singing his accursed song.

"How's he getting away? In the rowing boat, by God!"

Then, in a flash, everything became clear. Perhaps he had seen a living soul and was trying to save it.

A living soul around here, when the *Dermond-Nestle* was wrecked nine days ago?

"Hm! I must be deranged. You need to keep an eye on your boiler, my son. It's bubbling over, and all this solitude doesn't do you any good at all."

Indeed, it was hard to imagine the predicament of someone who survived a shipwreck and landed on the back of the *Baleine*; he wouldn't last three hours there, standing up or sitting down. The only way you'd end up there would be if you were like a lump of soft cheese, a bundle of clothes that could no longer fight its destiny.

I leaned out, but the rain blurred the view in all directions, the lamps' rays were turning to yellow steam, and the reef was submerged over two hundred meters away from us.

The witch's voice was still moving farther away.

The old man's a good rower! I thought, resigned to accepting all his eccentricities.

At heart, I resented him for not having got the boat out on the evening of the catastrophe. That would have been the natural thing to do.

I kept watch for the rest of that dismal night, presuming I would never see Mathurin Barnabas again.

The next day at breakfast, my skipper sat down in front of a bowl of hot soup that I'd had the audacity to prepare without consulting him.

He'd returned from his nocturnal roam, not without difficulty, by the look of it! Oh, the poor old man, what a sorry face! He really was sulking! His head was sunk between his shoulders, his eyes were bleary, his cheeks were the color of wax, his hands trembled, and his whole demeanor was dirtier and shiftier than usual, a clear sign than his rescue hadn't been successful.

He ate his soup greedily, drank a glass of his tafia, then went to bed, mute as a fish.

For two days he kept his mouth shut, doing his rounds like a clock that chimes because it's been wound up.

Now that the dead weren't paying us any more visits, I arranged to take leave the next time the supply boat came. My replacement was always at the ready on the *Saint Christophe*'s poop deck. He would disembark, swinging from the hoist, and I'd be off.

I'd be carrying my notes about the loss of the English ship, a long list of tins of food, a record of plank numbers, and lists of lots of drowned people.

I was bursting with pride at having such a solemn mission. Misfortune dictated that I should spoil this little moment by playing about with a telescope up there on the gallery.

It was the day before I was set to depart. I was examining the area around the *Baleine* curiously. The weather was quite clear, the swell was calmer, and a warm breeze, a spring breeze, had paused to let the waves warm up.

The storms would come back, of course, for bad weather is also a habit that the sky never gives up, but just at that moment there was a breathing space.

I focused my telescope.

There was a white smudge on the reef's dark back.

It was a long back, several meters, rather like the keel of a boat upturned by a hurricane, a shiny sealskin.

Not a tuft of algae, not a blade of grass, not even a grain of sand stuck in a crevice. Just smooth rock, polished by the water since the beginning of time.

Across it, a livid body.

... Yes, a corpse spread-eagled there, legs to one side, arms to the other, and the swell swishing a sort of brown drapery around its head.

The body was completely naked.

I don't know why I felt suddenly feverish, seeing it naked.

It was so white, so pure, its bobbin shape so pretty.

"It's a woman!" I cried.

The brown drapery? ... hair ... very long, loose hair. A woman with no lifebelt, she was. A young woman decomposing in the warm June sun.

I wanted to cry and ...

I wanted to laugh, the nasty laugh of a boy mocking the shame of naked girls.

I ran down the spiral staircase to find the old man.

He was on his way to prepare the docking crane, the supply boat being expected at any moment. He pulled his hat down over his ears and made his way toward the esplanade, bent double, a bird of prey dragging its tattered wings along the rocks. His harpoon trailed behind him like a long, bald tail.

I brought him up short:

"Captain!"

"What now?" he growled, with a start.

"There's another body on the back of the *Baleine*. *This time it's a female!*"

I don't know what the old man must have heard in my voice, but it stopped him in his tracks.

Suddenly he straightened up, became very tall, not his usual hunched self, and his eyes flashed, lighting up his pale face as he gesticulated madly, his harpoon at my chest:

"All right, there's a woman out there. And she needs to be left there, my boy."

"The ebb tide will catch her and bring her round to us this evening, Monsieur Barnabas; in any case, we'll find no clues on this one, she's naked from her head to her toes, the poor lady."

"The tide'll bring us nothing at all."

"Why not? It's funny it hasn't done it already. It's been three days . . ."

"What?"

I waited. I had my reasons. I watched the old man, still brandishing his harpoon at me, and saw that as I gazed at him he was changing color.

Finally the terrible weapon fell from his hands.

"You saw me in the boat that evening, didn't you?"

"Yes, I saw you, Monsieur Barnabas. So brave . . . when it was too late to save anybody!"

"She was dead," he whispered, in a wrecked voice, "so no harm looking."

"She was naked too . . . It's very strange she can't seem to get off the reef . . ."

As I asked my questions, I seemed to be explaining things to myself. All sorts of dark things.

"What of it?" he sniggered, caught in my trap and stunned by the scream of the siren announcing the supply boat. "You're not thinking of denouncing me? I'd have saved her if she'd been alive, poor little minx. But she's nearly rotten . . . so . . . *what did it matter? . . . I fixed her there with two hooks.*"

"You filthy pig!"

We stood there facing one another, paler than all the drowned corpses in the sea.

We understood each other at last . . .

The *Saint-Christopher*, belching out steam, turned its left side round to us and called out with the loud hailer, as it always did.

Without a word, our arms moving in time, like laborers who always worked together, we threw out the buoy. The pass rope was caught and attached to the hoist, and the crane was lowered, as the little steamboat let off white jets and whistled loud enough to burst our eardrums.

"Ho! Heave! Heave! Heave ho!"

Moving like one person, we heaved on the cable.

"Heave ho! Heave! Heave! Ho!"

The parcel of provisions came over, then the replacement keeper, another parcel wrapped in tar cloth that we had to dry out and cheer up with a glass of rum that I *gave* him myself.

And then it was my turn. I hooked myself to the hoist and flew over to the *Saint-Christophe*, where I was met by a friendly bunch.

I could tell them, in all truthfulness, that I hadn't seen a human being for six months.

I cried with joy.

That made the officer smile.

VII

I had a wild time, oh yes, a real party! One chore after another! Running from office to office, harpooned by one, reeled in by the next . . . and a third one asking for every last detail of the wreck . . . as if I knew the first thing about it!

What I did know, I'd resolved not to tell.

In Brest nobody was talking about anything except the sinking of the *Dermond-Nestle*. They went on and on, bewailing it—there'd been huge losses, it turned out.

When I'd finished my reports, signed all the bits of paper and told them all about everything I hadn't seen, I had twenty-four hours left to have fun. Twenty-four hours in six months!

What a party! I drank a bottle with an old traveling companion I came across in a tavern in the port next to the arsenal, and we made each other sad with stories of our troubles. But I had money jingling in my shirt pocket. A few solid silver coins. I told him stories in which I did my best to convey the dignity of being the new lighthouse keeper.

"A tower owned by the State, my friend, where you're all set up, your own boss, you see!"

He nodded.

"True, true, that's fair enough . . . but hearing the wind caterwauling . . . you don't look well, Maleux."

"Well, of course . . . there is the wind . . ."

I kept pausing, leaving long silences between my sentences. I was struggling to talk like a normal person.

Those months of hibernation had rusted my tongue. I found myself slurring, almost imitating the old man's quaver. I couldn't loosen up anymore. I felt as though the paving stones were rolling under my feet. I couldn't eat, couldn't drink—and I'd promised myself a hearty meal of omelets, bloody meat, and green salad. What tormented me was the idea of time, weighing anchor and dragging me back to the deck of the *Saint-Christophe* the next day at dawn.

Should I go and find some girls? No! Not now ... I'd never leave. And if you miss your return trip, the substitute takes your place. They don't joke around in this bit of the navy. And anyway, I was keen not to have anyone else question me about the wreck of the English ship. I was fed up to the back teeth with the thing!

Twenty-four hours!

What to do?

"You could walk out of the town," my pal suggested.

My pal was right.

Take an excursion in the wide-open spaces, stride over solid ground, see some trees, smell the scent of gardens, meet some men, maybe some women. We left the tavern.

"Jean Maleux," said my fellow traveler, "It's been good to see you ... I can't come with you as I've a family dinner to go to, but I'll shake your hand most sincerely and ... good luck, because you're settled to your satisfaction."

We shook hands. I didn't dare ask where they called home, his family. If he'd thought to invite me to dinner, I'd have paid my share with some bottles for dessert, one good deed deserving another, as it goes, only he didn't think to. To him I was a Monsieur, the stoker.

So we parted ways, hearts heavy.

RACHILDE

I wandered about, completely disoriented. And it was a Sunday, the streets were full of children. I was in a daze.

I'd been so set on having a good time, forgetting the toil and the old man, especially the old man!

I wandered off, hands swinging limply at my sides, out of town toward the headland by the *Minou* lighthouse. Instinctively, I gravitated toward the tower.

I walked with my head down, eyes stinging, gazing fixedly at my feet tramping along. That was the only thing that brought me any pleasure. Bit by bit, I came out into real countryside, where cliffs dropped off steeply around the old fort covered in meagre, salty grass; there were spindly trees, open-air cafés painted with patterns of leaves, a bit more grass, thicker and more like real grass, a few rocks, cows grazing, and, glimpsed between the hills, a drab, steel-blue horizon: the sea again.

I was near the lighthouse now, in front of a small, isolated house. It began to rain. It rains all the time in Brest, even in June.

That was the last straw. I was wearing my new clothes, my navy-issue overcoat and my waxed cap. I couldn't face rushing back into town. I thought I'd go into this hovel and ask if they knew of a little dog for sale. If I put it in with the parcels of provisions, it wouldn't be too heavy once its paws were tied, and we'd be hoisted up to the *Ar-Men* together, even if it made all the sailors on the *Saint-Christophe* cry with laughter. I swear, I wasn't thinking of having a good time anymore. It was as though I'd had a spell put on me. It was wiser to think about serious matters and get your house in order, even if that meant you might never leave it again.

So I went in.

Around Brest, all the houses serve food and drink, and keep a few groceries in stock. They sell what they can. This one was very poor and very small, with a few jars, a poster for Menier chocolate, and a bottle of Pernod displayed in the front window.

Inside it was almost clean and smelled of fresh milk. Sand was sprinkled over the red floor tiles. A few tin pitchers shone on the dresser, and a bunch of lilac in a butter pot adorned the counter. The landlady was nowhere in sight, but she'd left her knitting on a chair. I banged on the counter. An old lady came in, emerging from an invisible staircase. I bought two bars of chocolate and a reel of cotton.

"You wouldn't happen to know of a little dog, Madame? A puppy that I could rear?"

"No, I haven't any dogs here. There are some around, from time to time. Won't you have a bowl of something while you wait for a break in the clouds?"

"In this weather, I won't say no. I'll wait and let the rain stop."

I sat down at the counter, near the bunch of lilac. It was ugly stuff, its sparse flowers already wilted, but to me it was a sign of the spring I'd missed in my exile. I breathed it in ... as though it were the word of God.

The landlady served me some cider and busied herself opening up the doors. There was a smell of stables. A cow was standing outside, and as I wasn't chatty, the old lady went back to her milking, leaving me to admire the bouquet.

What a way to spend my leave!

I was dozing off, seized by an irresistible urge to rest, not wanting to drink or speak, my legs already giving way from having walked a couple of miles, my arms heavy, my ears buzzing, when I was woken by a young laugh. Someone was making fun of me. For the sake of my dignity, I took hold of the lilacs and took another sniff.

"Well then, don't be shy. Break some off! It's not dear at the moment."

I turned around like a guilty thief. My eyes met two female eyes and fell into them.

A girl of about fifteen, quite tall for her age, in a pleated skirt with a velvet bodice and a white shawl over it.

Her black hair was parted in the middle and combed flat. She had a short, straight nose, a mouth that looked mischievous, or perhaps just mocking, and a face covered in freckles.

"You're very kind, Mademoiselle," I replied, embarrassed, "I'd gladly break off a little piece."

She obviously found it funny to be called Mademoiselle, because she made that movement that all children do when you make a mistake in front of them, dipping her head and hunching her shoulders.

"Nobody'll mind if you take it all—we were just going to chuck it outside. We've got a tree of it in the yard."

"I'd like to see it," I said, politely.

She burst out laughing:

"Aunt!" she bellowed, "Our customer wants to see the lilac in the yard."

The old lady shouted back from the stable where she was milking:

"Well go on then, Marie, show him."

I followed the girl.

The yard was up against the side of the cliff. Six square meters of sand and gravel surrounded by a gorse hedge, with a shelter on one side piled willy-nilly with bundles of twigs and kelp, garden tools, and heaps of cabbages. The tree, which was no more than a bush, bloomed in the northern corner, if you could call it bloom-ing: its gray leaves and aborted flowers flourished like a rash of spots.

"There it is," the girl said, her eyes laughing as she affected a serious expression, "But you can play boules out here, too."

We went over to the boules. Half the shelter was set up for customers, but there nothing in the way of greenery, just the usual rustic table and pair of benches. We sat down.

Opposite us was the wall of the house, which was growing moldy in the rain. The joys of nature!

"Are you not from around here?" the girl asked, blinking her brazen eyes, having a good laugh at her aunt's customer.

I must've looked like an idiot.

"No . . . I mean . . . I suppose I am, Mademoiselle."

And I began to smile a little.

We chatted about this and that, the *simply horrible* weather and the gales to come. I was still mortally afraid of being interro-gated about the great wreck. She didn't ask me once. Perhaps she hadn't heard about the disaster. I learned that the *Minou* lighthouse was popular with visitors from the town and even foreigners.

I gradually got better at following what she was saying: she spoke very fast, in a short, clipped accent, not like the girls from Brest who have a sing-song way of talking. When she paused, her fingers fiddled with her shawl, a nervous gesture that contrasted with her assured tone.

Feeling more at ease now, I plucked up the courage to ask her if they could give me dinner there.

She became very serious.

"It all depends! If you're picky . . . we've got potatoes with bacon, and a leftover bit of fried meal. We can do that with some milk soup or an omelet."

"I'll take that happily, as it's raining so hard . . . Oh, anything suits me you know, Mademoiselle."

She ran off to tell her aunt.

I heard them rejoicing together, and the old lady said:

"Get him to wait while I strain a cheese."

Marie brought me a small glass of cognac.

"But you're going to get me tipsy for sure, Mademoiselle!"

"My aunt asks you to *await* for a moment. This is on the house."

"I accept . . . on one condition: I'd like to offer you a glass too. What do you say?"

She replied brusquely:

"No thank you, I don't drink that stuff."

"It's poison, is it?"

She laughed again:

"Maybe we wouldn't give it to you if it was, even for free."

"Oh, and what about with some sugar?"

Her eyes lit up.

"All right then, just for the sugar."

She finished my glass in a few sips. And she began to tell all sorts of girlish stories, in which I managed to make out that her aunt often scolded her for going *on the run-around* in the streets of the town.

"We never get to go out, here. On Sunday after mass, I have to stay here all on my own, to *await* customers who don't come."

Alas! The poor girl! There were still some who came . . . Only, she was such a young thing, my God! And I was in paradise just looking at her.

She couldn't know that I'd just left a hell behind me; her little freckled face, her cheeky mouth, her wicked eyes—they all beckoned to me and pushed me to be brave. Feeling her so close to me,

I was almost proud, finally finding a happiness that didn't immediately die away. I had no bad intentions. I only wanted to rest my eyes on her eyes. It gave me confidence.

They were beautiful black eyes, a little sly when they glanced sideways to see if the old lady was at the window, and so curious, full of innocent vice when they let mine gaze into them.

The rain was falling and so was the evening. The scent of lilac spread around us, a sad little scent like powder on a servant's hair.

"Tell me, Mademoiselle Marie, have you not got any sweethearts?"

The girls in the inns around Brest aren't ignorant of the word love from a young age.

"Well! My aunt would make a terrible fuss . . . I still go to catechism, Monsieur."

"What's to say you can't do both?"

"We'd have to know each other . . ." she replied, coldly.

She knew exactly what I was getting at.

No, she really was too young. I couldn't marry her. I couldn't . . . it was stupid to indulge in pointless temptation.

"Come, Mademoiselle, what are you thinking? . . . I was only joking . . . and I'm not from around here . . ."

She glanced over to the house furtively, then leaned toward me:

"Would you give me a gold cross, a real gold cross like lovers give each other. Would you?"

"With pleasure!"

We were still joking, but it was too dark under that shelter.

We could hear the butter sizzling in the aunt's pan. She paid us no attention.

I lowered my voice:

"Are you from here, a real Breton-speaking Breton girl?"

"Yes! What about you?"

"I come from the hospice in Brest. I've no family. But I'm assistant keeper on the *Ar-Men* lighthouse, and that's not a bad position . . . we should see each other again . . ."

"Is it far away, that place?"

"A hellish long way! I can only come off every fortnight, and only if the weather's good, you see . . ."

"So you're a sailor are you?" (She pulled a face) "A rogue, then!"

"Who's told you such terrible things about sailors?"

She tittered:

"I've got a friend, the little Tréguenec girl, the rope-maker's daughter . . . *they* got her with child and went off and left her . . . she's in the hostel now, you know!"

I was embarrassed. I looked down.

"You know some nice things. How old are you?"

"I'm not fifteen yet. If we come to an agreement, I'll tell you a secret."

"Let's come to an agreement."

"On the day of the gold cross, not before."

I'd have liked to make a run for it, but it was already too late.

Her aunt called us from the door:

"It'll be ready shortly. Be patient! I'm rinsing the lettuce."

And she disappeared, her headdress pushed far back on her head.

I rested my forehead on my hand:

"Do you think you could find me a dog, a nice affectionate puppy? I'm so alone at the lighthouse," I said, after a *brief pause*. My voice was very different now.

"Oh, if only you'd come earlier! They killed one yesterday at Jeanne Barroy's place, a tiny one whose mother couldn't feed it anymore."

I knew it! It was too late . . . for the dog!

"Is something the matter?" she said, seeing I'd gone quiet.

"Yes . . . I'm never very cheerful . . . My life isn't good . . . You can't understand . . . you . . . you're a child . . ."

"I can't be a child if you call me Mademoiselle."

I shook my head and tried to smile. She put her little brown paw on my shoulder, her nervous fingers fiddling with the cloth of my coat just as they fiddled earlier with her shawl.

"Come back on Sunday! We'll go for a walk by the sea, and I'll comfort you, if you have troubles."

"Oh no!" I cried, "Not the sea! . . . never again . . . I can't stand water . . . it smells of drowned women, the sea does!"

"What? What are you talking about?"

"It makes me ill to think of the sea, little Marie!"

"What an idea! Think of me . . . I'll give you some lilac to take away with you."

Wine . . . and lilacs to go! That should be the sign on the door.

I grasped her wrists roughly:

"If you had any idea of what it means to be lovesick, you wouldn't be so jolly. Love leads to abominable things."

"Does it now? Best not to do those things, then, isn't it? I know what I'm doing."

"Marie?"

"What is it now?"

"Look me in the eyes."

"I'm looking at you, aren't I?"

We were silent, hand in hand. She stared at me like an insolent boy—she really was more like a boy than a minx—but she accepted the first challenge of love, because since her friend, the little Tréguenec girl who was two years her senior, had made her mistake, Marie was burning with desire to resist somebody. A funny little idea in the head of a child who was either free in her thinking or twisted.

"You're pretty, Marie."

"That's not true," she replied, disdainfully.

She really didn't care!

"Give me a kiss."

"No!"

"Yes!"

"I don't know how."

"D'you want me to teach you?"

"I don't know you."

"We'll get to know each other. And this is the best way."

"And . . . what about the cross? A real gold cross, you know."

"Do you want me to give you the money to buy it tomorrow in Brest?"

"That might be best . . ."

"You little b . . ."

The word didn't come out, luckily.

I saw her eyes shining in the dim light, like a child who's about to cry.

And they were glowing, too . . . *like a cat's.*

"*Like cats!*" Just what the little Moorish girl from Malta used to say, except she was from Marseilles.

Perhaps Marie had understood. She added, more flirtatious now:

"I'll give you some lilac from the tree . . . and I'll wait two weeks . . . no longer than two weeks . . . or I'll forget you."

"And what if I never come back?"

"I won't be a bit surprised, you know!"

It was already a battle. She had the same system as all females: defending herself at all costs and only accepting . . . down payments. I felt drawn into the game.

I tried to force her to kiss me.

She gave me a good thump in the chest and with a sudden leap—oh! her skirts didn't hold her up—she escaped me, running to the house.

I couldn't retreat now. I followed her. I had my system too . . . It was to be as polite as anything.

The dinner was excellent. My appetite was returning, and I ate heartily. The potatoes with bacon had a delicately charred flavor, and the cheese was very fresh and smelled of cream.

The aunt trotted back and forth, very attentive, happy, a poor little blind woman glimpsing the shining sun of a yellow coin.

The girl snorted with laughter every time the old lady turned her back, and she stared at me, her eyes fixed on mine so brazenly that I was afraid. She was like a little animal irritated by someone pinching its skin underneath.

It wasn't me pinching her. I sat next to her as good as gold, all my attention focused on refilling her glass.

I would have loved to sleep in that house! The old lady explained that it was too cramped, and the cow lived in the old room they used to rent out.

"When you leave, you'll find plenty of inns on the other side of town, and there'll be lads there to wake you up in good time for your boat."

I paid my bill: three francs and ten sous, and I asked Mademoiselle Marie very timidly if she'd keep me company a little way with me, as she liked walking so much.

"Oh!" said the aunt, "She'd be outside all the blessed day through. It was raining today, otherwise ... you'd have seen her run off ..."

Marie put on a clean apron of soft silk, and a tulle shawl. She didn't wear a headdress, but she neatened the velvet band around her flatly combed hair.

At first, we followed the path without speaking, then I took her arm and put it under mine. She was very small and trembling. It's always a solemn moment, taking your first sweetheart.

"You're afraid of me now, Mademoiselle Marie. I won't do anything to displease you, I swear."

"You won't try to kiss me anymore?"

"No, I'll make do with the bunch of lilac ... that you forgot to give me this evening!"

"Oh yes, the lilac! That wasn't polite of me ... I should have ..."

"It makes no difference, seeing as we're not going to come to an agreement."

We were walking along by the ditch, which seemed even blacker next to the pale road.

"What's that? Is there somebody over there?"

She squeezed up close to me, her voice faint.

"Where? I can't see anyone at the entrance into town."

"I won't go any further with you, Monsieur Jean Maleux, because of the lights."

"Goodbye then, Mademoiselle Marie."

"I'll see you soon, then?"

"What for? It's all one or all the other. You're perfectly free and so am I. Better leave it there ... perhaps we'd be unhappy."

With a sudden movement, just as when she'd leaped backward when we were sitting under the shelter, she threw herself into my arms, standing on tiptoes to reach my face.

Our lips were united.

Oh, that girl was born knowing how to kiss, I swear it! She gave herself completely, offering nothing but all the ardor of her mouth. That was all she knew, but she offered it like a little piece of heaven.

Her eyes glowed like two lamps.

I seemed to be drinking wine from a brimming glass, slowly at first then faster, so as not to lose a drop. We stayed there, our mouths pressed together, for almost an hour, not saying a word. It was a Breton kiss, the king of kisses, which intoxicates chaste lovers . . . or kills them!

VIII

As I stepped back onto the base of the *Ar-Men* I felt I'd returned from a long voyage, even though I'd only been three days away from my sad house.

I was returning from a long voyage because I'd touched hope. I wasn't returning alone: I had a woman in the depths of my eyes, and my lips still carried the taste of her first kiss.

Yes, I wanted to be a man, I wanted to be happy. I gave away happiness in great handfuls as soon as I was back in the prison, gave them to the young keeper who was going off, hanging from the hoist, and to the old man who examined me like a wary animal.

This monster's personal affairs weren't my business anymore. I hadn't denounced him to our bosses, and now his madness no longer frightened me. *I felt saved.*

Or at least, I told myself that certain fears should be reasoned with, that I should be able to tolerate the presence of a poor doddering old man.

Evening fell.

We lit the lanterns: up above, the shining crown of the lighthouse, down below, the little smoking lamp for our dinner. And, once again, we sat down opposite one another, not saying a word. The sea's great moan rose up, surrounding us with convulsive sobs (she always cried without knowing why). And it felt to me like the lamentation of a betrayed wife. There's nothing you can do about it, but it makes you angry. She was moaning because I'd been away, the trollop ... Three days' leave in six months! She reproached me for fleeing by singing me an angry lullaby. It sent me to sleep and put me in a bad mood. She lulled me, or rather, she fooled me. I didn't owe her anything.

The old man cut his bread into large lumps and swallowed them quickly, gulping them down his saggy chops like the monkeys in the Brest Zoo.

We were eating cod in oil.

He served himself: first some oil, then, bang in the middle, a drop of petrol. I burst out laughing.

"What?" he said, "It seasons the sauce. I can't taste the vinegar anymore."

"You're going to poison yourself, old shipmate," I said, affectionately.

"Rubbish!" he replied, shrugging his shoulders.

He didn't ask for news of our officers or news from land. He was completely indifferent to the wreck of the *Dermond-Nestle*, and now here he was replacing vinegar with petrol to cheer himself up.

We filled our pipes. The smoke thickened. The silence around us was as heavy as a cloud full of lightning.

Would the storm break this evening, tomorrow evening, in a month, or a year? And we said nothing, thinking terrible things.

The old man pulled on his hat to climb the spiral staircase, and I noticed that the decorations on it were different. The two spaniel ears had changed color. He was wearing hanks of brown hair instead of blonde.

I didn't think much of it and blamed my sudden nausea on the thick air of our dwelling.

Where in God's name had I seen those long brown tresses, all damp, shining and dark at the same time, as though dipped in oil?

Our cod oil.

I didn't sleep well, that first night back in the *Tower of Love*.

But what did the old man's eccentricities and the sadness of the sea matter to me?

I'd met a woman!

For nearly a week, this was my store of joys. I didn't dare talk about my hopes, for fear of being mocked. I kept them hidden deep inside my chest like birds, except these birds never fought in the cage of my heart. They huddled up there, preferring the warmth of my body to the daylight outside. They cooed, repeating pretty little phrases over and over, their fluttering wings befuddling my movements. When I was out on the gallery, the wind smelled of lilac, and when I went down to eat among the foul smells of the lower room in the lighthouse, a hint of fresh cream haunted my mouth.

Love? I didn't know it existed before I suffered this waiting. True, she was too young, but she'd surely wait for me, and she'd love me better for knowing me better. Two more weeks of toil then I'd see her, and she'd tell me all her little troubles, her girlish stories, her sweetheart's dreams. There was no going back, upon my word, for either or us; we'd got engaged over there in Brest on the road to the *Minou*, next to a dark ditch, so dark that she pretended to be frightened of it, the sweet little tease!

Love? Gradually, this skinny little girl grew and grew, towering over the sea. She rose up in front of the lighthouse, she came to me, lifting the white tulle of the foam to make herself a new shawl. I'd give her gold crosses . . . and metal shone on the waves, glinting in the summer sun.

She was beautiful, far more beautiful than shipwreck women, naked, their hair spread out behind their bodies.

I found I'd also started humming, little tunes with no beginning or end.

Because the young fool in love is the same as the old fool who remembers.

And they both die a little each day for having waited too long.

One evening when a west wind was blowing, Mathurin Barnabas was securing the crane, which was threatening to collapse, when his cap was lifted off. He scrambled down the outside rungs as though he'd had a sudden fit of vertigo, and ran to the bottom steps of the landing, where he leaned over and nearly slipped into the raging water as it tried to wrest his horrible hat from him, only to surrender it in the end, covered in gobs of spit.

"By God and his saints!" he roared.

I watched him from the top of the iron steps. It couldn't possibly be the same man. His green-tinted eyes had lost their dead fish stare and were fixed on the wet cap in a warm caress. His hands, his octopus tentacles, wiped it with trembling passion.

He climbed back up to the crane, knotting his handkerchief lovingly over his brown dog ears.

"You're very attached to that . . . creation, aren't you, father Mathurin?" I asked him, forcing myself to laugh, because there were few enough chances for that.

"What creation?"

"Why, your dog ears, with the greatest respect!"

"I haven't got a spare cap here," was his only answer, which wasn't an answer at all.

The old man's cap was becoming an obsession. I saw it at all times of day. When I first arrived, he'd only worn it at night, possessed by a mania for the blonde tresses. Now, he never took off the long dark tufts, always keeping them shining and wavy with sardine oil. It gave him the look of a hairdresser's doll, except that hairdressers don't choose death to adorn with false hair, but the heads of young women . . .

Another week passed quietly and slowly over my brimming heart. I was singing inside. The birds of my love were trying their wings, and I hid my gaiety so as not to rouse the monster's anger against them.

The evening before my leave, I gave in to temptation. As we were eating our evening meal, getting toward dessert, the time when you start to ponder, I said:

"You know, Captain Mathurin, it's too lacking in the fairer sex, really it is. I think I'll marry soon. May we know your view concerning marriage?"

The old man gazed at me fixedly, chewing on his bread. He began to cluck like a chicken.

"There's no need to make fun of your comrade," I said, offended by his manners.

We were laying slices of cheese on our bread, and our knives shone harshly in the soft grease of rotten milk.

The wind groaned at the doors, a prying wind, like an animal poking its panting muzzle into all the cracks and breathing its fatigue inside.

We were tired too, of keeping our secrets.

I would have liked to breathe love into all my words.

The old man blew death over the table, and it seemed to me that our cheese was turning green, rotting under our knives.

"Maybe . . . maybe not," he grunted between mouthfuls.

That encouraged me.

"You see, skipper, it's no life! I can't resign myself to waiting until I get my promotion. Anyway, it's not money that's the problem. If you're not rich, you can always find someone less rich and make them happy. And as it happens, I think I've found a good match: an innkeeper's girl. A real Breton girl living at the very edge of Brest. A young kid, my word, and a skinny thing, but they grow fast. We've come to an agreement. One more year and she'll be old enough to marry, and I'll get used to a visit every fortnight. The navy prefers us to get our affairs in order when it comes to lasses. I can't go a different way every month, you see … first the girls on the arsenal side, and then the hussies over on the prison side. No, it's not hygienic … And as for having a mistress, when you can't pay well! … All things considered, a real woman is a more honest setup, and it suits the profession of keeper of a State lighthouse. Do you see, Monsieur Barnabas?" (And I added, with a touch of melancholy) "I've no family except you … so it's as though I were asking your permission."

He grunted, chewed, swallowed, and finally said:

"You'll be a cuckold, boy."

"What an idea! No more than any other man, I don't think."

"You'll be a cuckold."

And he sniggered.

That made me very cross.

"Old Barnabas, you don't know your duties as a father. I'm young. I need consolation."

"A woman is a bad thing *in a couple*."

The old man really was mad. What did he think went into a *couple*, if not a woman?

"Drowned women aren't my cup of tea," I declared, getting up and steeling myself against a possible punch in the face.

He didn't flinch. Just clucked:

"Oh yes, women stick to you like glue," he muttered, "and out here they don't show their ankles so much. It's maddening. I've seen a few, I have, I've seen some beauties, young ones, short ones, tall ones … all the lads from here would bring them back in their shirts after they'd been on leave … and then they'd go and wash their shirts . . . like you . . . they were delicate . . . and then they'd put aside their shirt like you will one day, so as to be nearer your skin, because our skin's the best . . . and in the end there they'll be, you and all of them, in peace, waiting for high tide . . ."

I stared at the old man, my fists clenched. I was ashamed for him, for his madness. You'd think he was standing plumb straight, but the first swell knocked him into the sea. A purgatory invented especially! And I had to live his life with him, listen to him . . . Even when he wasn't talking, I was afraid of him.

"Monsieur Barnabas, you've never had a wife? A real one?"

"Maybe . . . maybe not."

There was a long silence. He'd stopped eating and was wiping his knife on his leg, his head down:

"It was so long ago," he added, in a voice that was almost natural.

I seized my courage again.

"Tell me that story . . . father Mathurin."

"No point. You'll get to know it yourself in your turn."

"You should still . . . warn me. It would be more comradely."

I went over to him and put my hand on his shoulder. I had more pity than respect for this strange sort of a skipper who, on the navy's orders, I had to follow up and down all the steps of the lighthouse. I only wanted to clean up his heart a little, just as every morning, as an act of kindness, I polished the great pile of sardine tins he stacked up on either side of the fireplace.

He shuddered and raised his dead eyes, which suddenly glowed with a phosphorescent light.

Even putrefaction manages to shine once in a while, and all the drowned souls that the sea hides in her blue belly sometimes make her eyes gleam when the breeze softens or the swell is warmer.

"Are you a tattletale, Jean Maleux?" the old man snarled, with a reproachful look.

"Father Barnabas, if you were my age, I'd ask you to step out onto the base with me. That's three times you've accused me of being a spy, and I won't stand for it a fourth time. I can't stomach it."

He got up and seized his hat.

"It's time to keep watch. Marry or don't marry . . . it's none of my business. I keep the tower. All you need to do is keep out of the way of bad luck. I'm going up. Are you coming?"

He placed his hat carefully on his head, folding his black dog ears, his wolf ears, over his human ears. Now he looked older and younger, mingling the look of his own drunken old woman's face with that air of a coquette off to a ball who concocts a ridiculous hood for herself so as not to spoil the hairdresser's creation underneath. It also reminded me of a Black woman I once saw in Algiers, running through the dirty streets with a bandage on her face because she'd had some teeth taken out. The odd thing was that Barnabas reminded me of her because of the black hair over his pale cheeks, whereas she had a white handkerchief over dark cheeks. I was turning into a lunatic just looking at him, the old lunatic! There must have been some kind of sorcery in the atmosphere of the living quarters.

"Think what you like, old man," I muttered crossly. "Even so, women do stick to you some days, even though you're wearing . . . mourning for them."

I didn't dare say: wearing their hair, and in any case I wasn't sure.

He shone a pair of candles out at me from under his lowered eyelids, but he didn't reply.

I followed him, gnawing angrily at the crust I was still holding in my hand.

He climbed, tacking from side to side with even steps, very slow but not unsteady. The only old thing about him was his old lady's face. He was still a man when it came to work, and he never once lost his head when he was on watch.

He was humming: he couldn't climb without his little song, dammit.

As he was holding the lantern, I could see his silhouette dancing over the walls. It seemed enormous, already climbing right up to the lamp shining from the very top. I could only glimpse his legs in the turns of the spiral now, and still he climbed, headless, with a heavy, supple movement like a huge climbing beast, cut in half.

Halfway up he stopped and turned, his face suddenly red, splashed with all the blood of the light.

He sniggered:

"Women? . . . I could cure you of them if I wanted to, just like I cured the other one."

I shivered in spite of myself.

We were level with one of the lighthouse windows that he'd blocked, because (as I thought) of his rheumatism. It formed a sort of boarded-up cupboard in the thick tower wall, a wooden door closing up the window space. The window itself was sealed on the outside with a sturdy grating and thick glass.

"There's women here," he said, giving the cupboard door a fierce kick.

The blow resounded horribly up and down the spiral staircase, the slightest shock making the whole tower vibrate like a brass horn.

"Skipper, it wouldn't be permitted for you to hide them . . . the rules don't allow it, you know that full well! And anyway, how the hell would she have got up here? . . ."

I didn't have it in me to joke, chilled as I was by all his insults.

"Well, I've never seen that rule. There's a woman here . . . But I don't open up for her anymore. The joke's over with that one."

And he sang under his breath:

It's the tower of love!
. . . of love . . . ove . . . ove . . . ove . . .

You might be a man out in the daylight and the sunshine, even by moonlight, but in the evening, after a bit of cheese, when you've had time to ponder and an old so-and-so's been swearing at you, and you haven't been able to ease your feelings by slapping him in the face, you're not so sure you're in charge. My reply was curt:

"Don't play clever, Barnabas. God is closer to the sea than to the land. Might hear you. There aren't any policemen here, but the thunder can come down on you."

"It won't get in through that window, my lad, you can be sure of that. Mathurin's word. It wouldn't dare . . ."

My teeth chattered. What on earth had he got in that cupboard?

I ran my finger down a groove in the wooden shutter. It was a solidly built door, made of oak with a steel frame. We know what we're doing when it comes to strong locks in lighthouses, because a storm can tear a shutter off a wall like a knife shelling a walnut, and when the window was open the wind would have been enough to tear the guts out of the staircase.

The old man raised his lantern.

"That's one'll never make me a cuckold."

And he started laughing, an abominable laugh.

"Now look, father Mathurin," I begged. "Don't try to make yourself even nastier than you are."

"What? I'm a decent man . . . I don't bother women and I don't break the rules. I got myself married a long time back, and now nobody, my lad, can cheat me anymore. They're better girls than the others, and they don't talk . . . *butter wouldn't melt in their mouths*."

I passed in front of him, my stomach turning over, with not the slightest desire to ask him about his second marriage. I was suffocating. On the gallery, surrounded by the dazzling flame of the light, I felt calmer.

The old man was clearly raving.

We held up our lamps; a furious wind swept across our faces and flogged the old man with the silken whips of his hair. He looked like a jester at a village fair. His thin, red mouth, sagging inwards, performed strange contortions, and his glittering eyes wept pinkish tears. His burning gaze reflected the light in drops of blood. Either he was just a poor madman . . . or he was the devil incarnate.

I picked up a bird that had fallen down the side of the glass, a swift, still twitching after its plunge into the fire.

"Here's one that won't believe in midnight sun anymore," I murmured, just to say something, because the old man's ferocious eyes were filling me with horror.

"Same for you. When you've fallen in the sea, you won't believe in love anymore, little lad," the old man said, very calm.

"Captain, you're forgetting to crank up the regulator."

I stretched over to adjust the mechanism and closed the pane over the ferocity of the flame.

"All right, all right," he muttered.

"All right now," I declared.

He went back down alone, leaving me in my room.

... Tomorrow! Tomorrow I'd see her, the girl I only knew by the taste of her lips! I'd go back to her tomorrow, and this time there'd be no pile of papers about the wreck to hand over so I'd have my whole day's leave. As soon as my feet touched land, I'd go to her house. Her house! Marie! It was a bit of luck that her name was Marie. I liked that name. We'd soon make plans. I hadn't stopped thinking of her for two weeks. I felt her close to my chest. She knew what we'd say to each other tomorrow. She knew it already. We'd stayed in each other's arms, hadn't we? And anyway, we take people as we find them, no need to keep stumbling blindly on. We wanted each other just as we found each other. Two kids, more or less! I knew just about enough to make her happy, in the end. The old aunt with the little shop wouldn't half giggle with happiness when she heard me asking for her niece's hand, and for a year we'd go where the wind took us ... I'd be appointed head keeper instead of Barnabas at the *Ar-Men* ... or somewhere else ... and we'd have children straight away, the same size as their little mother. Here's to a happy life!

I felt so kind and good, so tender, so honest.

And I glanced at the little Moorish girl from where I sat on my bed.

"You were very nice, I'm not saying you weren't. Only you did drink too much tafia and you plucked a sailor like I'm plucking this swift. Pretty? Not as pretty as my fiancée, even though you thought you were prettier. You wanted some odd things ... and I was almost ashamed. I'm a gentle soul, I am. I like children, simple, naïve people, who believe in God and want a holy ring. Girls who like sailors aren't right for a nice, well-behaved boy from the ships

... who's lowered his anchor now in a State tower. Oh yes, she was very nice ... the little Moorish girl."

I finished plucking my bird and put it on a shelf to wait for the roast I'd make with it the next day, before the *Saint-Christophe* went off. Then I went over to the Moorish girl.

It was a scrappy little photograph that had cost me a few sous, covered in dark spots and crumpled from sitting in my pocket, but it meant a lot to me all the same, because of that lovely tipsy day we'd spent on Malta, on the blue water, like a dream.

The Moorish girl looked a bit like Marie. A bit ... a lot, really. She had her dark, sly eyes, and except for her hair, cut short like a cap on a little hooligan, she held herself in the same teasing way, with the same liberty in her smile.

"They're both full of vice," I thought to myself gaily.

I had no vice at all. I wanted the best of their love. That was impossible with the first one because the glass had already been emptied many a time, the glass of her red lips, spiced with a lewd smile. But the second one would keep all the pure wine of her caresses for me, and to her I'd be a tender, playful brother who'd only ask for what was allowed ... for a bit of play ... until the wedding night. Yes, my wanton little Moorish girl was like Marie, my intended. Two pretty bodies, two young, playful brunettes. I compared them to one another, but only knew one well.

Their bodies? ... My little Maltese friend had a round mark just there, a black lentil. It was so round and so black, that mark, on her milk-white breast, it seemed detached from the skin like a little star floating in air, a little star floating in fluid and swimming, flying, toward tender lips.

That bosom, that mark ... all that whiteness and the sign of mourning ... Where had I seen white like that before, and a sign of mourning, long, flowing back like a widow's veil?

"The drowned woman! By God! The drowned woman on the reef!..."

As I dropped off to sleep, I peeked at the photograph of the Maltese Moor, and I thought of my pretty little fiancée, but . . . but it was the drowned one who sucked at my marrow from the depths of an atrocious nightmare, the old man's drowned woman who had me completely, body and soul.

Because the mysteries in our dreams are warnings from God.

IX

I turned my beret round and round with clumsy fingers, lost for something polite to say.

I'd sat down near the old woman, who was mending stockings, and lowered my voice to tell her frankly all about the impatience that was torturing me.

"I'm sure you can see," she said, "In this weather we couldn't tie her down at home! She's gone out, my niece has. She's a little run-away—needs to put some distance between her and home before she can sleep properly!"

I hadn't imagined, before that morning, that you could be so simply unhappy.

If I hadn't got myself onto a chair near the old lady, I'd have gone crashing down.

It pinched my heart, enough to make me swear.

I had a gold cross for her, bought from a real jeweler in Brest. Not any old tat, a solid cross, and a galette with candied fruit tied up in silver foil. Engagement presents.

She . . . well, she'd gone out . . . to run around . . .

"She didn't mention . . . anything?"

The old lady looked at me over her glasses.

"No, nothing . . . Did you ask her to bring something for you? . . . Or perhaps you wanted to eat here? Heavens! I wasn't expecting you, so you'll have to make do with something simple."

"Won't she be back for dinner this evening?"

"I don't know. When she goes off with her friends, sometimes they all go together to see my cousin. He sells fruit in rue des Bastions. Then he keeps an eye on the whole gang of them. It's cherry time now. One basket more or less, you know . . . But she'll come home, Monsieur Maleux. Nothing bad ever happens to that child."

The old lady knew nothing, saw nothing. She was deaf and blind. Anyway, how could she have guessed there was a serious lover inside this sad boy wrapped up in his one obsession?

She didn't spend her life stewing in a deserted tower, where the true life-saving light seemed to be the love of a young girl. No, she couldn't understand me or approve of me. Her niece wasn't old enough to marry, and if she did hanker after love, it was as a little girl did, a girl still young enough to be running around the streets. She'd forgotten all about the poor sailor who'd washed up on her doorstep one rainy afternoon. There was no malice in it. On land people come and go, and one passerby makes you forget the last. She'd jumped into my arms then, and now she was jumping over the skipping rope with her cousins. When she came home, she'd burst out laughing or fiddle with her shawl with her little wandering cat's paws. Oh, it was all natural enough. I could have cried.

In my disappointment I didn't mention the cross, and I crumbled up the cake and ate it, to prove that I wouldn't eat the old woman's food. Should I leave straight away? Once I'd gone, should I come back? I felt a stranger to everything and everyone.

My God, how I suffered!

The little shop hadn't changed, only it seemed terribly dirty to me now, poky and dark, thick with smells of cows, sour cream, and poor cooking.

I had to get out of there and never come back . . . never . . . I said a curt goodbye and left without explaining myself, trying to look proud. No need to tell Marie I'd called.

We wouldn't come to an agreement at all. And as there was no shortage of women, I'd find another who was more serious when it came to promises. I walked along aimlessly, not thinking to go somewhere else for a meal, and went and sat by the sea.

"You'll come back and see me. We'll go for a walk by the sea, and I'll comfort you, if you have troubles."

That was exactly what she'd promised.

A cruel child? No, just a child.

I threw myself down on the grass where the land sloped down to the seashore, pretty grass like velvet, looked after by gardeners. I buried my head in my arms, wanting to sleep in the full midday sun. There were all sorts of rustling sounds around me, Sunday trippers passing by on their way to the *Minou* lighthouse; there was laughter on all sides, and a girl in a pink skirt went back and forth on a swing behind a pretty cottage . . . swinging between the lilacs.

I tried to reason with myself.

You don't set up your whole future on the first girl you come across.

Yes, but it's always the first one you love when you're in sore need of love.

And as for getting married in a year . . . better to marry today. I had my pay in my pocket, and it was my right, even my duty, to have some fun now.

Maybe so, but I wouldn't have fun now. Something squeezed my heart and my stomach. I cried. I couldn't stop crying.

"There's a chance to see her again in two weeks. We'll make up and come to a proper agreement. I'll go for a walk alone by the sea, and the next time we'll be together . . . she's so young!"

I managed to make excuses for her. An infinite sadness rose in my throat, a whole tide of tears held back too long.

I didn't love this little girl from Brest any more than I'd loved the little girls of Malta. I loved . . . Love!

Woe betide those who love Love!

Because they'll always be betrayed: even if they're loved passionately, they're never loved enough! They think infernally complicated things are very simple, like fidelity and tenderness, for example, or the passion that consumes itself in waiting for a fiancée or a whore, the passion that grows even as it is eroded away, that wants everything and then wants nothing because it fears to ask too much, the passion that dares nothing in the brightness of joy, because it has dared so much in the shadow and silence of torment.

Girls? No. I was dead to girls.

I finished off the engagement cake for my evening meal and returned to Brest, discouraged, wounded, hopeless, at a loss, friendless, not even hoping any more to meet little Marie along the streams that ran by the rue des Bastions.

I wandered around, looking at the shop windows. Oh, there were some nice pretty things for little Marie—dresses with trains, hats with feathers, and glittering jewels! Despite my sadness, everything led back to her, and without her nothing was interesting. The man who loves love is possessed by a demon who constantly shows him a loving face. Marie was lying in wait for me among the silks, under the lace, behind the most impossible diamonds. Hers was the body, quite naked, that my mind dressed in all those enticing fabrics. She'd follow me, admire with me, then suddenly she'd leave me, round a corner, vanishing through a door opened by another woman I didn't know. I had no thought of buying myself any sort of frippery. I went on as if drunk, wanting nothing . . . Oh, just to hold her hand in my hands . . .

And if I saw her, I was no longer sure I'd cry out: *there she is*, because I could only remember her dear little face the way it was one evening, full of desire, lit by her burning eyes, a woman's eyes for the very first time.

If I had met her, I'd have discovered a different child, a skinny girl like any other, with a sly look and freckled skin.

Perhaps I walked past her without realizing it.

So . . . I was right not to look round.

It wasn't her!

The next day, after a heavy night's sleep in the depths of a hostel full of rowdy sailors drinking punch, I set off again on the *Saint-Christophe*, bringing nothing with me from Brest except a little soil wrapped in a handkerchief.

"Aha!" called the chief stoker, starting to get familiar. "Someone's been out on the town, haven't they? In you get, old lady! You've got sacks of coal under your eyes!"

"Yes," I replied meekly, "I'm all in. I've had my fill."

I couldn't have been calmer if it'd been the day after my death.

. . . The light! My God, the light already! Here's the tower . . .

It's the tower, beware!
It's the tower of love . . . o . . . o . . . ove!

The waves roar, the crane squeals, it's raining salt, the wind is a hot, devouring breath. I'm falling back into hell . . .

"Ho! Heave! Heave ho!"

"Hello father Barnabas. We need to get on watch. There's a wind getting up, I'd say."

"So what if it's blowing? . . . You're talking rot. The light won't fly away without us."

He eyes me up and down, with a look in his eyes like a fierce, suspicious animal. He's wary of me because every leave I take might mean he'll be kicked out. He still thinks I've denounced him to the authorities.

But why would I denounce him, after all? For one thing, I'm not a tattletale, a spy trying to ruin his comrades, and I couldn't care less about his barmy stories.

I'm too full of sadness now to be worrying about other people's sins.

Anyway, was making love to dead women really . . .

(It's odd how sadness makes you want to blaspheme, and turns your judgement upside down . . .)

. . . I needed to take up my oar in the galley that never moved and stop dreaming of skirts.

"Come on, Jean Maleux, buck up! Nobody dies of love . . ."

All that day I joshed myself inwardly like that, often giving myself great slaps with my own arm:

"Look here, Maleux, are you mad too? A girl you didn't know from Eve . . . A runaway, a kid, who still plays in the street? A nice chit of a fiancée! Were you expecting her to keep house for you, look after the children, wait for you faithfully for two weeks and have hot soup ready when you came home! You must admit, Maleux, the *wind madness* has got to your mind! In any case, you marry when you're head keeper, not when you're the servant of a pig wallowing in muck like that Mathurin Barnabas, may the devil take him! . . ."

I did my duties as best I could, going through every detail of the job scrupulously in an effort to absorb myself in any kind of work, but I struggled. I wasn't interested anymore; I was too far from the world, too far from life, from its walking, talking, laughing, scolding reality. I was a hermit, and the worst thing was I couldn't manage to be alone, I wasn't free: the old man was always at my heels like a beast stalking its prey, still convinced that I was about to betray what I knew about his dead lady friends.

Or . . . about the murky business of the cupboard, the blocked window halfway up the stairs, a hermetically sealed door to which he certainly had the key.

Now my curiosity was tormenting me to open it . . .

You have to remember the state I was in. It's far from a normal existence when you live in a tall, narrow prison (like a cursed candle) and you've no choice but to mull things over there, not knowing what to do with yourself, too near the stars one minute, too near the chasms of the sea the next. It was thinking all the time that dismantled the mechanism of my intelligence. Never, never, had I ever had so many bizarre thoughts turning over in my mind. A sealed cupboard in my house? A fascinating mystery! From the top of the spiral staircase to the bottom there were six cupboards in all, each mysteriously closed.

Now, if I wasn't to open them from the stairs, nothing was stopping me looking in from the outside! The lighthouse prickled with little iron rungs, and if you've got feet accustomed to climbing up rigging, it's easy to walk along an outer wall.

I didn't go though, having found a better occupation.

I was making myself a garden.

Oh, not an ordinary garden!

A little narrow wooden box that I filled with earth carefully brought over from my last leave. I sowed a few seeds, and a bulb I'd been given back in the tropics, that would grow as long as it had enough water.

I set the garden by the porthole in my bedroom.

Every morning, I came to check on my garden with an anxious eye, wondering if any green shoots . . .

Ah yes, green shoots!

It was the sea pushing up green shoots, the furious sea, constantly lifted up like the breast of a woman enraged by love.

I skipped my leave that fortnight.

I didn't even want to go and find my lass from Brest anymore, and the girl I'd thought was my fiancée a week before now seemed distant, a trick of my imagination.

I should have persevered with my resolution to marry. That was salvation . . . but something inexplicable was taking hold of me. Giddiness, *wind madness*, or an appetite for suffering. I felt so sad, so pitiful, that I wanted to be even sadder.

And also, I must admit . . . Hadn't the old man predicted it? . . . *I'd already stopped wearing a shirt to be closer to my skin . . .*

. . . Oh, *Ar-Men*! Oh house of love, sweet house, dreadful jail, cradle of everything shameful, cellar filled with the troubling wine of solitary drunkenness, sweet house of aid to those shipwrecked in treacherous seas, truth of human light mingled with the stars' falsehoods, sweet tower of love . . . Our union came as does a necessary evil: the evil of living for yourself.

You no longer think of sin.

You no longer dream of pleasure.

Life carries you off in its current and throws you, broken at last, onto sleep's dark shingle.

Who broke the lonely man, so tired of being alone?

It was life, implacable life.

Who rocked the lonely man to console him for a while in rest?

It was death, implacable death!

And when we wake, we watch grass grow, searching for hope . . .

But grass doesn't grow in little coffins full of soil.

All that had bloomed in my garden was a few grains of salt, a gift from the ocean, a bouquet from the siren.

One night, when I was on watch, sitting near my window, I was assailed by visions of strange phantoms.

The moon was pouring pure, cold light over the waves.

The lighthouse, throwing its pink rays around it, was trying to catch the moon in its vigorous arms.

It was a strange combat between *Her*, the great virgin, and *Him*, the monster from the shadows.

She advanced, her face pale and very calm, driving back the golden mist that tried to reach her and make her lose her reason to shine.

Little by little, *she was eating him*, and making her own light out of him.

This process, the work of a dumb beast or a dissolute woman, could be clearly observed, because the bottom of her face was split by a shadowy mouth. She carried a wound there, a scar, or more likely a pair of lips that open every month and suck in the willpower and good sense of poor men.

The lighthouse reared up, gigantic, like a threat to the sky, brandishing itself, colossal, straining toward that dark mouth, the black rift in the celestial brightness, drawn on by the supreme duty to be as great as God.

And the golden mist rose and fell, reflecting blood, sucked in or driven back by the heavenly body with its seemingly impenetrable mask.

... How beautiful this pure moon was, fallen pearl, severed head, shining from another's pleasure, but never saying anything of it ...

And the lighthouse, in the howling wind pealing out for the diabolical nuptials, in the wind weeping with joy or singing with terror, the lighthouse seemed to strain even further, driven mad by the irradiation of the impossible.

Was it better to be extinguished?

Its right was to shine, to live ...

Flare still higher?

Human destiny is to burn where we stand.

... And the moon, fallen pearl, severed head, proud of the absence of its body, moved off, moved off demurely, chaste and distant, inaccessible, taking with it the mystery of a mute mouth that, perhaps, does not exist ...

... Oh tower of love, put out your fire! Here is the dawn!

X

Is it Easter, is it Christmas? The days flow, flow, unchanging, dripping into the sea like water, like tears, like the best of my blood.

When the *Saint Christophe* arrives with its baskets of provisions, we signal that the assistant keeper won't be coming off. The assistant keeper likes his work. He's full of enthusiasm. I think he'll be owed a decent burial if he dies on the job. Only the assistant keeper . . . doesn't give a damn!

He climbs up, he climbs down, he passes the old man climbing up or down, and the old man hums. Jean Maleux hums too, aping him.

We eat, we drink; the lamp is lit, the lamp is put out.

My God, is it Easter, is it Christmas? I hear bells ringing.

I'm plagued by habits. They're like magpies, always repeating the same nonsense, tugging at my sleeve to show me a point on the horizon, always the same one. It seems normal to carve grooves in the table with my knife while the old man counts the sardine tins piled up on either side of the fireplace.

It seems perfectly natural to me to wear away the button of my jacket by polishing it with my nail for hours on end, so that now the button's split in two and my nail's rubbed away to the quick. I do it mechanically, not neglecting the slightest detail of my work, and I don't believe I'm ill.

I'm certain now that the old man hasn't lost his reason, it's just that the long days spent immobile staring at the dancing sea, silent before the roaring water, have made him obsessive. He tried reading, to take a walk in another world, and realized he'd forgotten how.

It's not that we talk more, it's that we understand each other better, enduring the same hardships without really knowing why.

Hardship? Not a bit of it! We're worthy keepers of a State tower, entirely our own masters. We're rich.

That's the most terrible thing. Outside of our watch times, we're our own masters. We can dream, sleep, drink (because there's alcohol here, and good stuff, too), we can play cards and tell stories. We generally prefer to go back to our lairs, his down at the bottom, near the petrol tank, mine up at the top, near the lamp room.

What would we say to each other?

I don't take his ideas about drowned women seriously.

And he despises me because I had the idea, one morning, of marrying a *living woman* I didn't even know.

As for his ghoulish jokes about cupboards, they don't intimidate me a bit. He wanted to frighten me because he knows I have a *certain faith* in God.

And the ship's apprentice always needs breaking in—terrorizing the new boy by sending him to look for a corpse in a cupboard trains him up. I chose not to look for it, I'm too pigheaded!

My nights are ghastly. I see horrifying faces pressing at my window. White ladies, mournful under their long black hair, beckon me to follow them, then turn me cold with their dead eyes full of green water; as soon as I rise to follow them, they retreat, frightened of me as I am of them, and flee sadly away, long hair flapping on their backs, and I'm coward enough to beg them to stay.

My dreams are no longer filled with living women. I long for more passive, compliant creatures to amuse me now, far above worldly modesty. Or properly debauched girls, familiar with the true secrets of love!

And I'd also like to be able to throw them into the water, have my body free of them forever, never meet them on my path again.

My path?

I climb up, I climb down.

Sometimes I go down to the base and cast some lines, trying to capture a monster, a huge rot-eating fish.

It varies the menu. All the salted meat makes our gums bleed, and when the sea's rough we're often without bread.

Once, I dared say to the old man:

"Don't you ever go off the lighthouse then? Haven't you got anyone to visit on dry land?"

He replied:

"The only way I'll leave is feet first. And I hope, Maleux, that I don't peg out in summer . . ."

"Why, Captain?"

"Because if I died at the end of the two weeks, that wouldn't be so bad, but at the beginning . . . you'd have to keep me . . . until I turned to *mush*! . . . There'd only be one thing for it: drench me in alcohol!"

I'd never thought of it that way.

The old man decomposing in his hole while I'd be lighting the lamp up there, making it burn like the fires of hell, because our duty, alive or dead, is to burn to save others. We must be consumed here to deserve a place in heaven.

One day I asked (and our conversations stretched over weeks, a few syllables each mealtime, letting our thoughts ripen in between) how the young keeper, my predecessor, had left, feet first of course.

The old man grunted and turned his back on me, on the pretext of going to fetch his rum.

He won't ever talk about the *accident*.

Is it Ascension or is it Assumption? Which feast day is coming?

Pale mist hangs in the air, the moons are brighter, and from the sea there rises a more ferocious small, a wild smell that I've managed to untangle, as a dog knows the scent of its master approaching. It's the ocean in rut, the spring tide promising a storm. You couldn't say it's warm, because the air's still like a whip and the wind is howling, and the waves leap up and drench you with salty rain that numbs your bones when you're out on the base, but it's *blurry* weather. The water roils as though it were in a boiler, and the spray spurts in great white, foamy jets. Like bunches of daisies.

The lighthouse judders and vibrates, seems to be drifting sideways, slowly at first if you look at the base, or very fast if you look out over the *Baleine*. The blackish reef pulls at it the way a magnet pulls an iron needle.

And the eternal waltz accelerates; the more the waves leap, the more the lighthouse spins.

It doesn't make me dizzy at all. I do have the distinct feeling, though, that I am dizziness personified, and that having finally got the knack of running without moving, straight to my own ruin, I am the very center of all catastrophes.

I carry all misfortunes within me.

My head is hot, my stomach burns, and my legs are always frozen, limp as cotton wool.

I walk in a dream.

When I light the lamps, it's not rare for me to forget to close the door in the lens.

I know full well I'm going to forget it. I start to do it, saying to myself:

"Careful now, Jean Maleux."

Because I talk to myself quite freely.

And I forget ... or I think I forget to close the door.

I get to the middle of the spiral staircase then climb back up again, swearing.

I stand flabbergasted in front of the plate glass door, closed firmly in its frame.

I didn't forget anything. I only lack precision in my movements, and I have to keep an eye on myself ... because if Barnabas didn't check all my doings, I'd always be making mistakes. The storm is upon us, the storm is within us! God protect us!

... We'd eaten heartily that evening, the old man and I, because we were pretty sure there was a gale brewing. We couldn't face all the demons of the air on empty stomachs. We'd had a nice fillet of cod, with potatoes fried in oil, tinned beef, red as hare pâté, a splendid English pickle smelling of mustard, and then dessert: walnuts, raisins, and figs. We'd each eaten two pounds of bread.

We were grown men, after all!

The old man tried out a joke from his repertoire:

"It's blowing strong ... Maleux! I bet my cap the thunder will bring us some ladies."

I answered brusquely:

"We don't need females here! It muddles up the work."

"All right! I know my own meaning! Maybe, maybe not ... I've checked the crane ... I'd say we dismantle it completely."

"You think we won't sleep tonight, then?"

"I think, my son, that it's a fine day."

He spoke a language all his own, the old sea wolf.

We went out onto the landing, holding on to a length of rope tied to a sturdy ring inside the room.

Despite this precaution we were almost knocked down one on top of the other. The raving sea was drooling, spitting and writhing about in front of the lighthouse, exposing itself, naked to the very innards.

The trollop swelled up like a stomach, then hollowed out, flattened, opened, parting her green thighs; and in the lantern light you could see things that made you want to look away. But she started up again in a frenzy, a convulsion of love or madness. She knew full well that the men watching her belonged to her. We were family, weren't we?

A pitiful clamor could be heard around the *Baleine*, cries that sounded human but were only the wind. It wasn't time to die yet.

The horizon was still black, a dense black like melted tar. Clouds swept by, tearing themselves on the tip of the lighthouse. Soon they would swathe the light in their dreadful velvet hood.

That would be the worst time for us because the poor boats pick up speed in those conditions, not heeding the forecast of blackouts.

Mountains of water rolled toward us from the *Baleine* as the waves hurled themselves at the rocks, rearing over them, crowned with the white flames of their spray, which on stormy nights seems to give off its own light.

And what a pleasant light, like the sheet thrown over the corpse when it's set between its four candles.

We were finding it almost impossible to stay upright.

The old man gave a snarl and dropped down to walk on all fours for safety.

He looked like a huge crab. His back was arched, his legs scraped the stone, and the pincers of his fingers felt their way over the slippery surface.

I pushed on from one iron hook to the next, clenching my rope between by teeth.

We were beasts.

Supernatural beasts: more than men, because we were battling against the heavens, and less than spirits, because we were no longer conscious of what we were doing.

We emerged from our shells to sniff out death and try to protect others from it. But we had no pride. We were beyond any kind of noble thoughts—we were too dazed. And we groveled before the sea, which split its sides in reply, cackling in our faces.

We took down the docking crane. We wound in all the ropes and folded down the hoists. The wind sank into us like an eagle's claws into a sheep's wool. We got so many slaps in the face, and they felt so *real*, it made us want to slap back. Sea snakes slid around our legs, and cold, slimy tongues licked us all over. Once the lighthouse was shipshape, we turned our minds to what was happening up at the top.

Shrieks and howls were hurtling up and down the spiral staircase, a whole string of devils pulling each other's tails and swearing, meowing like enraged cats.

Toward the middle of the staircase, Mathurin Barnabas paused to look at his precious cupboard of women. But he said nothing, and his eyes changed color for a moment.

That shook me more than if he'd joked about it in his usual nasty way. If he was looking at the thing *for himself*, perhaps there really was something in there.

He didn't point to the spot, contenting himself with remembering.

I stopped too, making a point of pushing the door to check it was properly closed.

The others were closed less tightly than that one.

We hurried on up the stairs and arrived at the gallery just in time to see the snuffing out.

A sudden black fog, stinking of petrol, covered the vast light, and not one ray fell on the water.

"What's this?" said the old man, annoyed, "It's turning bad. Go and get the torches."

In extreme cases, we fix torches all around the balustrade, and keep lighting them until the last one is carried off by the wind.

I went back down to fetch the torches and saw that the clock was showing ten o'clock.

This performance was going to last all night.

My little room high up in the tower, where it was usually very bright, was completely dark. I felt my way from one shadow to the next, the wind plucking at the lanterns in my hands and trying to hurl them miles into the sea.

The old man hadn't taken his cap.

He was probably too afraid of losing it, despite this being such a momentous day.

We lit the torches; they threw themselves overboard without asking us the way.

Once, I felt myself lifted into the air. The old man brought his crab claw down on my shoulder and folded me in two.

"Moor your foot!" he said, dourly.

I knotted myself a thick garter of rope and offered to do the same for him.

He shrugged his shoulders.

"That's for children!" he growled.

We crouched there like fiery statues, the light searing our backs and the wind freezing our chests.

When a more terrible gust hit from one side, the comrade on the other side got up and fetched a fresh torch.

But the wind rose up in complete revolt. There was an immense clap of thunder, the sea's belly swelled up to the clouds and tore itself open on a flash of lightning, and the noise deafened us.

"Ship!" the old man breathed, crouching next to me.

We had no more torches, we had no more petrol, the light had gone out, and the glass cage was flying off in pieces.

I couldn't see the ship yet, but the flashes of lightning revealed it to me for one second, as though it were daybreak.

A huge, dark-hulled ship, upright like a horse rearing on its hind legs.

It was walking toward the *Baleine*.

Its fate was sealed. No use warning it. It had been advancing to its end for over an hour, the ill-fated thing!

We heard no alarm bell, no orders through a megaphone, no shouts of despair.

The great vessel, like an enormous, stubborn animal, wanted to go that way ... it had decided. It slid along, still upright, rocking grotesquely. Now it was hesitating between the reef and the channel.

"They'll come right onto us!" I cried, terrified by the height of the monster. "They'll crush us!"

"No danger of that," replied Barnabas, whose eyes were flashing green next to me. "The *Baleine* steers them from underneath."

And he started to laugh.

The wreck of the great black phantom happened all of a sudden. Among the howling wind and the groaning thunder, we heard a din of planks, an abominable din of very dry wood splitting.

It was the big coffin gashing itself open on the back of the *Baleine*. Then it was finished. Everything disappeared, carried away by the current or sinking to the innards of the sea.

"May they rest in peace!" I stammered, tearing at my hair.

"And their women too," Barnabas added in a cynical tone.

It was dawn by the time the storm died down, and we went to bed, crushed with fatigue.

Luckily, we'd eaten well the night before.

At solemn moments like this, the weight of a meal keeps us anchored to the rock of existence.

XI

The next day, we had to patch up the damage. Even though we weren't one of those enormous floating coffins that transport living bodies, we were just as afraid of storms and lightning as they were. A piece of the frame from the lantern cage had broken off, pulling away one of the iron rungs as it crashed down the side of the light-house and opening up a crack in the exterior wall.

"Needs looking at," the old man declared.

He seemed weary and troubled, more tired in the brain than in the shanks. He was on the lookout for wreckage! . . .

He usually took it upon himself to perform the most difficult tasks because he was more experienced than I was, and also because he was always worried about my *tattletaling*, as he put it. Perhaps he'd forgotten what to do? . . . (after all, he'd forgotten how to read) or perhaps he was so consumed by waiting for . . . wreckage that he didn't have the strength to scale the heights again after the wild night we'd had.

Toward midday the sun broke through the mist and rain a little, and I climbed over the gallery railing on the south side. Tied on firmly with a rope around my waist, I climbed down from rung to rung, not looking around me as I was feeling pretty uneasy despite the good glass of rum lining my stomach. The old man claimed the damage was between the fifth and sixth windows. The piece of frame must have dislodged a rung above one of the windows blocked from the inside ... windows that he refused to unblock, under the pretense that it would take too long.

In any case, we had to inspect the outside for our report to the navy. A single stone torn out of this immense column could lay it completely open to the sea's assaults, and we'd collapse like a house of cards.

Hanging at the end of my rope, I hopped about grotesquely like a puppet, a little Punchinello on patrol around a bell tower. Between my bare feet, curled over the rungs, I could see a silk cloth spread out, either very close or very far away, but in any case so pretty, shimmering so wonderfully, that I could hardly resist the desire to let myself sink down onto it. The wind purred, tickling my neck and my ears. Now that the howling beast had devoured everyone, she caressed us tenderly and begged our pardon.

I saw that the fifth window was indeed damaged. The corner of its stone frame had come away. I pressed my knee against it and knocked down a lump of masonry with a whole rain of smaller stones. The grating over the frame hadn't suffered too much, but the glass window behind the bars was crisscrossed with cracks. My reconnaissance was complete, and all I had to do now was climb back up the rungs, tug on the hoist and write my report.

I don't know what demon tempted me.

I lowered myself down to the fourth window. It was almost in the middle of the building. It was ... the mysterious place.

As I climbed down, feeling my way, sticking my fingers into any suspicious holes, the sea seemed to rise up, bluer, greener, more shifting and entrancing than ever. She rolled underneath me, all innocence, casting chaste glances in my direction. On the last rung, above the fourth window, I leaned down, stretching out my arms to reach the next one. My rope was too short.

I should have stopped there. My curiosity, an unhealthy sort of curiosity, emboldened me. I wanted to find something out, because that day, for once, I had an excuse for finding something out. I was doing my job, and if I did it overzealously I'd hardly be reproached for it.

The old man was snoring in the lower room.

He didn't suspect a thing.

In any case, my pride wouldn't let me back down now.

Valiantly, I detached my rope belt, wound it around my wrist so as to have something to grab if I got dizzy, and bent down to the window until my forehead was level with the glass.

Then I let go of the rope and cried out.

I'd seen, yes, I'd really seen . . . behind the narrow glass mirror, another head, looking back at me!

I stayed clinging to the wall for a moment, my hair standing up in horror, my palms wet, holding on by a miracle.

I was mistaken, surely, or dreaming! It couldn't be possible.

Behind the iron grating the glass was intact, and it was misted up. It was as though there was water inside that window.

It was like looking into an aquarium where some rare monster swam.

But it was still possible to make out a mass of long, mournful hair, blonde faded almost to white, around the oval of a horribly sad face, the face of a young woman gazing at the sea, her eyes filled with tears . . .

As the sun caught the eyes, they shone . . .

I blacked out and fell, letting go of everything.

I pulled myself out of the ocean somehow. I'm a good swimmer. But tumbling into the currents around the *Ar-Men* means tumbling into death. I sank to the bottom, touched rock, then came up again, and I swear I was no longer thinking of the woman up there. I turned back into a fierce animal of a man trying to save himself, and I began to swim strongly, sometimes above the waves, sometimes below them, forcing myself to turn with the natural gyration of the current, not holding out much hope.

I reached the base and was rolled up onto the ramp before being thrown back down and then up again as the water toyed with me like a cork.

If the sea had been rougher, she'd have torn me to pieces, but she'd just had her fun and seemed tired of killing people.

I found myself standing almost upright by the north staircase.

Then my teeth started chattering. I gave a great shiver and fell onto the slimy slabs in a faint.

The old man nursed me. (What a nurse. My God).

I spent a week in bed.

He'd picked me up from the edge of the rock, not understanding why I was spread-eagled there, drenched, a heap of wet washing.

The rope, hanging from the gallery railing, revealed half the truth to him.

"Well," he said, as I opened my eyes, "That'll teach you to choose them too short, boy."

He gave me grog with pepper in it, an infernal remedy, and he'd have liked to add a drop of petroleum too, to spice it up, but I was too clever and refused to drink it. I was frightened of him, insanely frightened.

He was the one who *cured women*!

The doctor couldn't see me until the next time the *Saint-Christophe* was due to come. So nobody would know anything about my illness or my probable demise.

And I resolved to live, come what might.

So one morning I got up, and did my rounds as well as I could.

The old man looked at me mockingly:

"Up already, and looking lively! Ha!... always better to save your skin, even if you've got no shirt..."

He joked, circling around me and acting matey. Not one word about the lost ship.

The wreckage was invisible on the horizon, and (luckily for me) the drowned bodies had already gone out into the open sea. The old man, constantly on the lookout with his harpoon at the ready, said nothing of fishing out any beautiful girls.

It seems strange to say it, but the memory of that head glimpsed behind the glass gradually faded from my brain. My mind was exhausted by the eternal noise of the wind. I thought I'd been mistaken, had a hallucination, or a waking dream. I'd been through so many intense emotions on the night of the wreck! Hardly surprising if I'd gone a bit crazy. It could have been a strange reflection in the sunlight, the play of a shadow between the bars, my own reflection seen at a time when I was more nervous than usual, worn down by all the old man's ridiculous habits...

Now that I was seeing women in every corner, the best thing was to go to Brest, where there were real ones to be found.

And, after my lingering illness, I felt the inexorable resurrection of my virility.

We called out through the megaphone to the *Saint-Christophe*, saying that the assistant keeper would come off.

"Poor old lady," the stoker kept saying, "Poor old lady, are you not well?"

Our officer added more severely:

"You don't look good, Maleux!"

There was one street in Brest I didn't recognize even though I knew it well, because they'd done it up and built lots of new houses since my last visit.

It was like returning to earth after my death.

People had odd habits. The high-society ladies wore enormous sleeves like balloons, but when I'd last seen them, they still had normal arms.

Near the *Minou*, at the farthest tip of Brest, the hostel-grocery had been rented to two innkeepers, both men, who seemed even drunker than their customers, all dirty wharf rats in ragged clothes.

I went in, ordered some food, and asked after the previous owners of this seedy inn.

"Oh, old mother Bretellec went back to live in town. Set herself up selling fruit."

"And little Marie?"

"Little Marie . . . her servant?"

"No, her niece."

"Don't know her."

"A little brunette," I insisted, my chest tightening.

"Maybe she turned out badly."

They began to laugh at my embarrassed expression.

"It's not as rare as all that, girls turning out badly, my friend!"

I left, not daring to ask any more.

I wandered aimlessly like a lost dog. I had money, enough money to buy some good stuff, so I drank.

I chose a big café near the *Arsenal*, a very chic café full of officers.

I squeezed myself in behind a handsome pillar dressed in red velvet and crowned with golden hooks for hanging hats on. Very respectfully, I hung up my beret and got out my pipe. I smoked for a long time, my absinthe in front of me. I wreathed myself in clouds, and the greenish tint of my glass gave me a strange feeling: I was in front of an aquarium filled with murky water, and a melancholy face passed to and fro behind the clouded crystal.

To make the vision linger before my dazed eyes, I kept refilling the glass. Then I changed the shade of the water, adding redcurrant liqueur, brown spirits, pale brandy, and sometimes, to recreate a cloud, or mist over a rainbow, a little ash from my pipe.

Night fell. There were eclipses.

I found myself at the foot of the lighthouse, which had turned red, a bloody lighthouse crowned with huge golden spikes that pointed menacingly at me like sharp fingers; I tried to climb up it to get my beret, which was hanging from one of the fingers, but I could never reach it!

"Ho! Heave! Heave ho! I can't, damn it!"

And I made as if to wind the hoist on the docking crane. A waiter pushed me outside, having extracted a small fortune from me. I went off, humming the tune old father Barnabas always sang. Not happy, not unhappy either, not thinking about fiancées or whores. I went off, pondering over stupid things.

"Will it be sunny tomorrow? I could buy myself some soap . . . *How bored she must be behind the window, the head of the sea! . . .* No way of climbing up there . . . but what a party when we bring her down! By God, he's set himself up nicely, the old man! Blonde maidens in the navy prison . . . Enough to make the devil himself take up arms against him! I'd have a clear conscience if I did . . . we'll have to see . . . Toe the line, Jean Maleux. You were born under a lucky star, I tell you!"

In spite of myself, I drifted away from the rich part of town, toward the little streets behind the *Arsenal*. I knew the way by heart from when I used to take it when I was on leave from sailing with Captain Dartigues.

Was I really so much younger then? I used to be more eager to get there.

I was still young, only the sea had soaked me to the marrow with its melancholy, especially since I'd nearly succumbed to it, body and soul.

I went into a bawdy house whose door gaped open like the jaws of a ferocious wolf.

Inside it was all hung with red. The red hounded me, pricking my eyes with its thousand needles dipped in vinegar. I'd drunk it, and I was meeting it on café pillars, on women's dresses, in coach lanterns, and now on the walls of this house. It was soft to the touch, it was warm, it was good . . .

I heard whispering voices. They called me: *handsome boy*. I wasn't used to all this politeness.

I made to take off my beret, and realized I'd lost it.

A gaggle of fat girls made fun of me because I was looking around for my beret: they crowded around me, pinched me, slapped me on the back, lifted me up, put me down. What I did to them, I have no idea! The bawd got angry and threw me out.

I went into five other night houses like that, all opening huge red jaws to snatch me in, and in one tavern I met a few sailors who, already horribly drunk themselves, invited me to drink some more.

They were from the *Marceau*, a battleship about to set sail, and we sang a few mournful laments in her honor. Would the sea take her?

I kept seeing the great black horse of a ship that had been wrecked on the *Baleine* speeding past the lighthouse, and thinking of the authorities trying to fish it out from the Fromveur strait. As for its crew, nobody mentioned them anymore.

My brain was tormented by crazed ideas: declaring war on the sea, strangling the sea, cutting off her head.

I tightened my belt over my little Eustache knife. I could see something red pouring from the ceiling of the room where we were drinking.

Back in the street again, I left my new friends and reeled off, crashing into walls. My head was spinning madly. No more gas lights, no more carriage lanterns, no more lighthouses to be my saviors. I'd never get anywhere that night.

The singing, laughter, and shouts grew more distant. I was in a foul little alleyway, walking through sludgy mud that stank of the sea. I think it must have been a little backstreet near the fortifications.

I'll always remember that little alleyway . . . even if I live to be a hundred.

It was so narrow and dark that you wouldn't have recognized your own father there even in broad daylight. Up above, high up above, the roofs of the houses seemed to fuse together. A stream trickled by and, judging from the smell, it came from the dock where they mend boats, which is always full of dead cats.

There, too, doors opened and closed, snatching at nocturnal passersby, but the bawdy houses were less luxurious and in some of them the girls fleeced the poor sailors without even a government license.

I don't know why but I felt frightened all of a sudden, a fear I couldn't explain. I clutched my knife, clutched it as though I were marching into battle.

All the caresses the good prostitutes back there had given me, amid the torrents of red velvet, hadn't sated me or sobered me up; all the racket my companions had made, the sailors from the

Marceau, still rang in my ears like sounds of war. Who or what was I to fight? . . . And very far off, very high, higher than the houses merging with one another in the darkness, an electric light revolved, its white rays whipping the sky and dazzling me without lighting my way.

The most astonishing thing was that I thought I was at sea. I was going to the *Ar-Men* lighthouse, toward the *Tower of Love*, and I was crossing the sea on foot, no longer needing the *Saint-Christophe*. I could hear something walking behind me.

The patter of a mouse. The footsteps of someone concealing themselves.

"It's the old man!" I thought to myself!

It was all wrong to think of the old man, though, because it was a woman. She put her hand on my sleeve:

"Little man!" she said to me.

I was filled with a mad anger:

"Little man? Me, Jean Maleux! I'm worth three when it comes to carrying out my duties, and I've fought against the sea. You'd best not call me a little man . . . I've traveled too far!"

The girl, perhaps because she was as drunk as I was, perhaps because my words reminded her of a voice she'd heard before, suddenly threw herself into my arms, hanging on to my shoulders like an octopus, and kissed me on the mouth, a long, abominable, sucking kiss that stank of musk.

"That's the last kiss you'll ever give! The joke's over, dirty whore!"

And I stuck my knife into her stomach.

She fell to the ground. I carried on walking, not even turning back to look, walking with a firmer, more dignified step, intoxicated by an immense pride.

"What? I killed the sea!"

XII

Just another nightmare! That's what I kept telling myself for weeks. But I was tormented by the disappearance of my beret. I'd lost it in my crawl through the brothels of the lower town in Brest, and, still mindlessly rubbing the button of my jacket, I reflected that I'd have to buy another or . . . see the old one brought back to us in a police officer's hands.

It was a definite proof against me.

I probably hadn't killed anyone at all. Prostitutes are used to a few knife scratches from their seafaring suitors . . .

That one kissed just like little Marie did. (Another dream? How could little Marie, my fiancée, have turned into a prostitute and . . .)

I felt neither sadness nor remorse. I no longer thought or acted of my own free will.

And anyway, I'd been under the influence that night . . .

My beret never came back.

I sent for another one.

And weeks and weeks went by, months, Christmas, Easter, Ascension, Assumption. I heard none of their bells.

The *Saint-Christophe* came and went, whistling its call to life before the house of death.

I didn't answer, weary of trying to live.

We stayed there like two caged bears, the old man and I, speaking only when necessary for our duties and hiding our secret obsessions from one another, he declining steadily toward his end, not even studying the alphabet anymore, and I caught once again in the ferocious grip of an infernal force: the force of habit.

We ate and we drank, winding ourselves up like clocks every morning, ticking along wonderfully from dawn to dusk, and running down every evening after the first rays shone out from the lighthouse.

We did our duty of lighting up the world . . . blindly.

Duty is an obsession, the most terrible obsession, because you have faith in it. You think it'll save you.

The realization of my crime didn't really hit me in the guts until the day the old man collapsed on the lighthouse base, laid low by some strange affliction.

He was standing there smoking his pipe, leaning against the lighthouse wall, the spray spurting angrily up at him and wetting his feet.

I was on the north side, sitting on the parapet chewing tobacco and looking at him, surprised at how tall he looked.

Since I'd stopped speaking to him except in especially urgent situations, and since I'd repaired our crack in the fifth window alone by means of some cement sent by the *Saint-Christophe*, he seemed to bear a grudge against me.

But he still fulfilled his duties valiantly in stormy weather; and, after all, he'd warned me about the wind on the night of the wreck . . . We respected one another.

. . . Which wreck? I couldn't really remember.

All ships were wrecked around here.

We lived in the *Tower of Love*!

Mathurin Barnabas was tall. Thin and tall like the lighthouse. The only reason he stooped was to pick up the scent of wreckage.

His pasty face, his flat nose, his bloodshot eyes that now wept a sort of glistening mucus, and his high, bare forehead all made him look like a ghost of a man, a sailor perished far away now returning to torture his shipmates, perhaps because they'd sent him under too early with a ball around his ankles, just to get rid of him.

He was smoking, drooling all over his clothes, which were filthy and torn and had a foul smell coming off them.

He reeked of the cemetery.

I still kept myself clean. (Maybe I still liked myself a tiny bit). He had stopped liking himself, stopped liking his companions, stopped liking drowned women. He was just waiting for the last tide ... the one that brings the last boat for the last voyage in a wooden box. I reckoned he could well be sixty.

"Maybe! Maybe not!" he'd have replied, if he'd still been able to speak.

But now he only emitted strange noises, grunts like a wild pig that were impossible to understand unless he explained with a gesture.

He was smoking ...

Suddenly he pitched forward, his forehead hitting the slippery stones of the landing. He was about to be washed out to sea.

"Father Mathurin! Hey! Father Barnabas! ..."

I lifted him up, seizing his whole body in my arms. He was heavy as lead.

His legs were rigid, as if held taut by invisible ropes. His limp arms flopped around his body, making no attempt to find a handhold. Only his head was still alive, and his eyes, his poor abominable eyes glowed green.

"The boat!" he said distinctly.

"Which boat, father Mathurin?"

I wanted to talk now too.

My whole body was trembling.

I propped him against the parapet, ran to fetch a flask of brandy, and made him drink.

His teeth were clenched so tight that they broke the neck of the bottle, and he swallowed as much broken glass as he did brandy.

"Look here, father Barnabas, you can't go dying without your last rites . . . The *Saint-Christophe* came yesterday . . . It won't come again for another fortnight. What the devil . . . can you hear me, eh?"

He nodded and, to my astonishment, broke into the cynical laughter he usually reserved for stormy days.

All through to the evening I did my best to bring his legs back to life. They were worse than lumps of wood.

Paralysis, most likely.

I still held out some hope for his head, swiveling about on its neck. I pulled his cap firmly down, covered him with his old blanket that stank of fish oil, and left him alone for an hour while I went to light the lamps.

My heart pounded as I climbed the spiral staircase. His words came back to me:

"You'd better hope, Maleux, that I don't die in summer just after the supply boat's come and gone . . ."

I also remembered his odd recommendation to douse him in alcohol.

Anyway, he wasn't really going to rot for a fortnight right here next to me, was he, this old man who'd been rotting away in the charnel house of his own soul for so many years? . . .

No chance! I'd sooner throw him in the sea.

It would be a case of force majeure, wouldn't it?

When at sea, do as the sea does!

When I went down again, I found him lying there good as gold, stock still.

His eyes looked straight into mine, affectionately, and he said, in a tender tone that I'd never heard from him before:

"My poor Jean, I'm finished."

It was as though my father, my real father, had spoken to me.

I knelt down next to him and cried, forgetting my selfish thoughts.

"No, no, there's no need to frighten yourself, Captain. You'll start to feel your legs again. It'll take more than a fall, just a dizzy spell, to finish you off. At your age ... You've taken a knock, but ... look, I'm here to look after you ... We never talk ... but we understand each other, my poor old skipper. Misfortune has made us stand hand in hand for a long time now."

He tried to move but fell back and scraped the stones with his fingernails and the toes of his boots.

"Best put me on my bed, my boy," he said, his voice becoming clearer and clearer, "and rub me with petrol. It's a good cure. Try everything. I don't want to make things difficult for you, Maleux."

He was thinking about making things difficult for me, close as he was to his own death.

I was so touched that my tears flowed again.

My heart was dying with him.

Why, we'd lived nearly six years together.

Enemies? No! Only strangers.

"Father Mathurin, tell me what I should do. I'll obey you."

I dragged him along as best I could, a big talking corpse gradually coming back to its senses. I put him on his bunk opposite our fireplace.

He wanted a drink, and I offered him wine.

"No," he said, "Give me some water . . ."

He drank two mouthfuls.

"The water's bitter," he murmured. "Is it always like that here?"

He usually never drank it.

"It's all right, father Mathurin . . . usually. Do you want some sugar?"

"No, thank you."

And his eyes closed for a moment.

He'd said *thank you*! I didn't know how I could possibly repay him for being such a good comrade.

It wasn't his fault he was dirty.

It wasn't his fault he was nasty.

Something must have passed over him, extinguishing him and freezing the youthful vigor of his blood.

Poor soul . . .

It was as though his tall body, stretched out in the middle of our living quarters, was being crushed beneath the huge column of the lighthouse.

They'd imprisoned him there, and now he was carrying the heavy light with the last remaining strength of his human chest.

Now my younger chest would replace his, and I could already feel the burden crushing me. It didn't occur to me to try to get out of this duty, though.

When you stay put for a long time, you start to like the place of your suffering. It's more natural than going off to seek happiness.

I thought he wanted to sleep so I went and filled my pipe out on the landing.

It was a beautiful autumn evening, if you can call the sea beautiful when it's red, tinted by the setting sun as though by the fury of a fire. The waves rose and fell, so large and opulent in their luxurious silks and jewels that they put our poverty to shame. Oh, the sluts, the sluts! With all their little feline purrs, their roars like angry lions, their cabaret dances, and most of all the torrents of blood and tears that wash around them without seeming to leave a mark. Resplendent with all the liberties that men, prisoners of their desires, are forced to admire from afar!

We watch over them and they swallow big ships; we place our destiny in their hands, and they drown us between their billowing breasts.

The water played, chased itself about, bellowed obscene words and sang hymns, but most of all it was something that lived off the death of others.

The smell of the sea wafted inside on the pure wind, and it was an impure, sour smell, cracking the lips that tasted its exciting flavor, splitting the skin with early wrinkles and filling the eyes with salt, ready to make tears of despair.

The sea was beautiful, the sea danced in the setting sun and lifted the frills of its skirts over the lighthouse steps like a girl flashing her white underwear.

We'd soon be needing a white sheet, come to think of it, and it occurred to me that we didn't have a new one to make a decent shroud.

"Maleux?"

I turned round.

Father Mathurin had managed to sit almost upright in bed. He was getting paler, and his eyes were sinking horribly into his pallid face.

"Jean, you're a good comrade, though too young to bear all this . . . Jean, best make sure . . . I might go under . . . I can't feel my knees now . . . feel my heart . . . Is it still beating?"

I touched his chest.

"You're mad, old skipper. Nobody dies from one attack . . . it takes three. Anyway, I'm going to fly a pennant at half-mast and if a boat . . ."

He started painfully.

"The boat! The boat!" he kept saying.

"What boat, father Mathurin?"

He leaned over to look at the sea, as though he were really waiting for a sail to appear.

The sea was dancing again, but not a merry dance.

"There now, he's taking a turn for the worse!" I sighed.

I kept vigil with him, sitting completely still at his side with my arms folded.

The death throes were coming. He wouldn't see a third attack, and I'd be left tête à tête with a corpse, one that was completely dead this time.

A fortnight . . . and no way of burying him!

"God protect us!" I said out loud.

God must've been protecting us because he spared us a storm. The lamps up top shone peacefully while the principal keeper burned his last drops of oil.

Toward midnight, as I was coming down from the lantern, the old man seemed almost well. His eyes began looking around for me again, and his voice softened:

"Would you do me a service in the spirit of friendship, Maleux?"

I sat down on his bed and nodded.

"You wouldn't be scared?"

"I'm not scared of anything now," I declared firmly.

"Then . . . go and fetch her for me . . ."

I jumped up and cried out:

"Who? The woman?"

"Yes, the woman. As you've already seen her . . ."

My whole body trembled. He wasn't mad . . . I wasn't mad . . .

We'd both of us killed a woman we loved, when we were drunk with love or wine . . .

My crime, which had been buried in the depths of my mind, rose up again, and I saw the proof of mine in the certitude of his.

"Father Barnabas . . . I'm sorry . . . I thought I saw her head . . . one day a long time ago, behind one of the windows . . ."

"You're young . . . you don't understand . . . it's an old man's appetite, and . . . back then . . . the living one . . . she cuckolded me . . . I've never been able to love any except her, from pride . . . You need to go and fetch her for me and throw her in the sea when I'm finished."

He pointed to the leather pocket on his belt, which was always on him. I fished a key out of it, still warm from his flesh.

He signed to me to go.

But I was already off. I knew the way.

I climbed up, steadying myself against the wall, gasping for air and brandishing my lamp as though to defend myself.

About halfway up the staircase I stopped in front of the mysterious door.

Oh, no more mysterious than the other five doors on the five floors of the lighthouse.

I set my lamp down and put the key in the lock.

It opened very easily.

. . . Dust, a bit of sand, the fine, white, fluid sand that gets everywhere. No woman! No corpse, no skeleton; only, on the windowsill, up against the thick pane, half hidden in a greenish fog, a strange plant rooted in a glass jar, a large jar for storing fruit conserves . . . or poisons in chemist's shops.

This plant was spread around the jar in luxurious blonde shoots, smooth to the touch, very like hair.

As I turned the jar around, *the head* oscillated slightly, and its empty eyes filled with lights, glistening through the alcohol.

I threw my jacket over it, so as not to meet the eyes as I carried it away.

... With his crab claws, the old man caressed this hair pouring forth from its ring of cork in feathery cascades, then he said, very clearly, as I was hiding my face in his bedclothes:

"What, lad? Don't be a baby! ... She was beautiful ... I can tell you. She isn't now ... but you didn't ever see her body ... No other creature was ever so good for me, the poor abandoned fool ... she came like an angel when I was worrying myself sick waiting for the tide to rise. She came after a wreck ... dead for less than two days, not swollen up, not green, and so young, the poor minx ... and a virgin ... a wealthy young lady. She was caught by the hair on the boat's rudder ... such blonde hair, so thick ... (I took two tufts from near her ears, I loved them so much ...). They still had a scent of flowers ... flowers of the earth ... I kept her for one moon ... then I cut the head off ... *for my dessert of love.* Oh yes, very good, very gentle, very indulgent! But she made me kill someone, the one before you, a sensitive boy who only just caught a glimpse of her and killed himself. *He cured himself,* you see! Now ... you need to give her back to the sea. Because ... I'm a jealous man. Go on!"

I got to my feet; taking a run up, I hurled *it* from the top of the steps. The jar smashed, with a sinister sound of glass shattered by a fist, and the head, free at last, sank to the very depths.

When I came back, the old man was laughing an almost tranquil laugh, his powerful hands lying flat on his chest, and he'd stopped breathing.

He was cured too!

I recited the prayer for the dead that all seafaring people, whether they believe in God or give themselves to the devil, know by heart.

I recited the prayer for the dead in my immense solitude peopled by ghosts . . .

. . . After three days I doused him in petrol.

. . . On the fifth day I wrapped him in all his clothes and sewed him into his sheets, sealing him in.

. . . Around the eighth day I stopped eating, stopped drinking, and locked myself in my room. I blocked up the door to the stairs and spent my time outside in the sun on the gallery.

But I had to go down to fetch fuel for the torches in case of storms.

It was like a breath of plague rising up the spiral staircase.

My courage failed me. I had the sacrilegious idea of throwing him into the water, weighed down with iron filings and lead.

No! I mustn't . . . He still needed prayers. I mustn't . . .

I set him outside in his bundle in the northern corner of the landing.

This torment lasted for the prescribed fortnight.

Worms teemed over the bundle, gorging on human fat . . .

"Ship!"

I bellow and jump up and down with excitement.

It's the *Saint-Christophe*.

They send me over a comrade, the shore-leave stand-in.

And the authorities arrive: a very serious-looking officer, the captain, the doctor, and the priest.

The hoist brings them over one by one, first like ridiculous little puppets, then, when they get their feet on the base, bigger and grander.

I'm moved by the sight of all these compassionate faces, and I take off my beret like an honest man.

I'm a criminal before his judges.

I try to explain myself and I cry.

"Come, come, Maleux!" says the officer, "You're a good lad . . . you've been brave . . . yes, a terrible situation to be a fortnight out here with no help . . . You'll be rewarded! . . ."

He talks for an hour. My ears hurt. He makes us stand around this stinking bundle and informs us that it was a man . . .

"Thirty years of service! A good fellow, my friends. May his soul rest in peace. And that makes you, Maleux, the principal keeper."

The priest kneels.

We're all crying.

And they leave, grand at first, then little puppets dangling from the strings of fate.

"Ho! Heave! Heave ho!"

We hoist hard on the ropes, my assistant and me, cheered a little by having a drop to drink and raising a toast with the top brass.

I've been appointed principal keeper.

Marie, my darling little Marie . . .

Before God, if he's listening, I swear I'll never see land again.

XIII

So, since I'm scared of forgetting my alphabet too, I've begun writing my story in the great book of the lighthouse. I record wrecked ships, fishing boats passing by belly up, and, one by one, all my memories of love, sinking into eternal sadness.

But I do my duty despite myself.

I remain firm at my post.

The obsession with duty is the beginning of madness.

. . . And I am mad, hoping for nothing, expecting nothing . . . not even the drowned beauty of the rising tide! . . .

Melanie C. Hawthorne is Professor of French at Texas A&M University. Her work focuses on women writers primarily of the period 1850–1950, and issues of gender and sexuality. She is the author of *Rachilde and French Women's Authorship* (2001), *Finding the Woman Who Didn't Exist: The Curious Life of Gisèle d'Estoc* (2013), and *Women, Citizenship, and Sexuality: The Limits of Transnationalism* (2021). In addition, she has published a translation of Rachilde's *The Juggler* (1990) and editions of Rachilde's *Monsieur Vénus* and Renée Vivien's *La dame à la louve* with the MLA (2004 and 2021). Her current writing projects focus on the Anglo-French writer Renée Vivien.

Jennifer Higgins is a translator from French and Italian. She has translated fiction, drama, and poetry by such authors as Clara Schulmann, Maurizio Onnis, and Villiers de l'Isle-Adam. She recently produced the first English translation of Jean Lorrain's 1906 play *Ennoïa*. With Sophie Lewis, Jennifer has co-translated several works by Emmanuelle Pagano, including *Trysting* and *Faces on the Tip of my Tongue* (longlisted for the International Booker Prize), and she has also translated a number of nonfiction works on subjects including contemporary music and modern history.